Four Days with Hemingway's Ghost

By

Tom Winton

ALSO BY TOM WINTON

Beyond Nostalgia
The Last American Martyr
The Voice of Willie Morgan and Two Other
Short Stories

ISBN   1478160586
EAN   978-1478160588

Chapter 1

Other than my wife, I hadn't told a soul about it. I was afraid to. Nobody wants to be labeled a kook. Nobody likes being stared at from the corners of dubious eyes. But now, after all I've been through, I couldn't care less what people think. For reasons I will explain later, I am now sure that in July of last year, I spent four days with Ernest Hemingway.

Granted, Papa had been dead for five decades. I realize that. But a force far stronger than any of us mortals know did bring us together. Odd as it sounds, I'm as sure I was with him as I am that your eyes are narrowing as you read these words. Bear with me. If you will hear my story, I think you, too, will believe it.

To begin with, I haven't always been a Hemingway aficionado. Sure, I did read *The Old Man and the Sea* when I was eleven years old. But after that, like most young men on the lower half of the social ladder, the closest thing to literature I ever read was the sports pages. That was about it, that and an occasional peek at *Playboy Magazine*.

But then a funny thing happened when I was in my early thirties. I started making trips to the local library. And soon after that there was always a stack of books alongside my recliner. Since I, like Hemingway, had a great love for sport fishing and certainly didn't mind knocking back a few brews from time to time, I started taking a keen interest in the man and his work.

The more I read about him, the more I realized he and I weren't all that dissimilar. Oh, I never had the kind of money he did or a boat as fine as the Pilar. I never traveled the world or earned fame the way he did. But deep inside, I believed that along with our common interests, we had also thought along similar lines. Considering that our births were seventy years apart, and so were our worlds, I thought that our many likenesses were quite odd. I suspected that Hemingway, just like I do, would have had a serious problem living in this maddening twenty-first century world.

But despite all we had in common, I always doubted that, had I ever met the man, I would have actually liked him. I wanted to believe I would, but after reading so much about his overblown macho attitude, I didn't think so. In the farthest stretches of my wildest dreams, I could never have imagined that I'd someday find out.

Last July, I had to be airlifted from my home to a hospital in West Palm Beach after a highly-unlikely accident. I had just bought a utility trailer for my lawn care business and backed it into my driveway. The trailer was fully enclosed with a metal roof and sides. After lowering the tailgate, I set up a makeshift ramp using two wooden boards. I then cranked up my rider mower and tried to drive it up the incline. But it was steeper than I'd realized. After two failed attempts to get the mower's front wheels over the very top of the ramp and into the level bed of the trailer, I had to throw it into reverse and back the powerful machine down again. Going backwards on such a sharp angle was quite precarious. My better judgment kept giving me hell—telling me I shouldn't be doing this; I should drive over to Home Depot and buy two longer boards. But I didn't listen. It was a Saturday afternoon, and because we'd had a lot of rain all week, there were still three lawns I simply had to get done.

On my third attempt, I revved the mower up really high and sped up the ramp. Scary as it was, all went well until the front wheels finally did clear the top of the ramp. Just as that happened, I realized my head was about to slam into the leading edge of the roof.

It all happened so fast. Reflexively I jerked my head to the right, but that didn't help. Fast as I'd been driving the mower, it kept right on going, all the way into the trailer. It's amazing my neck didn't snap. Instead, with my head lodged against the roof and the mower continuing forward, I was literally pulled out of the seat—by my head.

And that wasn't the end of it. After the mower passed beneath my legs, there was nowhere to go but down. Back first, I fell between the two boards onto the concrete driveway. As the back of my head slammed onto the driveway, I heard a sickening thud like a gourd smashing against a wall. Then the lights went out. Everything went black. I didn't even hear Blanche's screams when she came out of the house to see what had happened.

I went into a deep coma and remained there for four days. No matter what the doctors tried, they couldn't get me to respond. My eyes wouldn't open. I did not respond to questions. I didn't flinch, grimace, or react in any way when they administered pain tests. I don't recall any of it. The only thing I do remember is spending those four days with Ernest Hemingway.

Right after I'd lost consciousness, a speck of white light appeared in the center of all the blackness. The glow spread quickly, and soon everything was bright and sunny. I was walking through a neighborhood of old but well-maintained homes. Some were small, some were larger, but they all were a mix of Bahamian and New England architecture. I was across the street from the houses, on a sidewalk infested with camera-toting tourists in gaudy tropical shirts. Right alongside me there was a long brick wall.

As if I were doing some funky, clumsy dance, I dodged and side-stepped one person after the next. I'd never seen so many belly-bags in my life and could not fathom how anybody could wear such a silly-looking contraption. But the strange thing was, as ridiculous as these people seemed, they were all giving *me* funny looks.

It was very warm, but the afternoon breeze blowing in from the ocean made it almost comfortable. Riding in on the wind was an exotic mix of aromas. As if returning from a long voyage, the soul-healing smell of tropical seawater was greeted and kissed by the perfume scent of jasmine and frangipani. Most every yard in the neighborhood was aglow with colorful flowers—red, white, yellow, pink, lavender, and multiple pastels. And the green fronds of towering palm trees rattled in the wind like frantic castanets.

With a dull ache in both the front and back of my head, I stepped to the right edge of the sidewalk, rose to my toes, and peeked over that privacy wall. Putting my hands on the top layer of bricks, I looked through the shade of the dense tropical flora. There was a mini-estate there. For the second time in my life, I admired the stately home with its airy, wrap-around porches on both floors. I imagined Ernest Hemingway, decades earlier, standing on the second floor portico looking out to the nearby lighthouse. Then I shifted my eyes to the right of the house, toward the shimmering aquamarine waters of the swimming pool. That's when I noticed somebody standing beside me.

The guy was right smack next to me, as if he were my date. I was just about to tell him to give me a little breathing room, but I didn't. He beat me to the punch. He spoke first.

"I hate that goddamned pool! Twenty-thousand dollars she pissed away on it. Can you imagine? That's two-and-a-half times what her uncle paid for the whole damn place—house *and property*."

Oh, wonderful! I'm thinking by now, *Here we go! I've got myself one of those burnt out Hemingway wannabes here.*

I was going to walk away without even acknowledging the guy, but I couldn't help myself. I had to take just one look at this clown first.

Peering from the corners of my eyes, I slowly turned my head. The first thing I noticed was that he was about my height—nothing unusual about that. But when his face came into full view I jumped as if I'd been goosed by a highly-charged, electrified thumb.

Jerking my chin in and my head back in one lightning-quick motion, my eyebrows sprung to my hairline. My eyes froze open—almost as wide as my mouth did. I shook my head—hard, as if listening for loose screws. Then I said, "My good God! *It is you*! Now I know I'm losing it!

Chapter 2

Ernest Hemingway was dressed just like you'd expect him to be. His powder blue Guaynabo shirt had long sleeves, and a knotted rope held up his khaki Bermuda shorts. Above worn leather sandals, his calves were still impressive, but that was where any similarities to the robust, macho Ernest Hemingway of myth and legends ended.

Just like his thick wide beard, the hair on his head was all white. It was combed down and to the side to cover his receded hairline. On the left side of his forehead, the scar he'd received many years earlier from a fallen Paris skylight was still plenty visible. It was the size of a healthy garden slug, and it protruded like a nasty, pink blister.

Bulging from his waist, was the same paunch he'd had throughout the second half of his life, but his once powerful shoulders and chest were somewhat shrunken. His face was old and craggy. There were liver spots beneath his sideburns and pre-cancerous pink blotches on his ruddy cheeks and forehead. But his eyes were different. They were the same dark brown they'd always been, but now, unlike after his late-life electro-shock treatments, they looked well-rested and raring to go.

"Yes, it's me," he said, eyeballing some of the tourists now. "But you'd better not let *them* see you talking to me. Look to the side or something. They can't see me, only you can. They'll think you're some kind of a nut job, Jack."

Jack! I thought. *He called me Jack! No, he must have been using the name as a figure of speech.*

"Surprised that I know your name, huh?" he said now. "Well don't be. I've been sent here for a reason . . . Jack Phelan. I'm not down here for a holiday. Well, let me correct that, I am here on a holiday but it's a working holiday."

"A working holiday? What are you talking about?"

"You're in a coma, Jack. As we speak, you're actually lying in a coma. I've been sent here to help determine if you should come out of it or . . . or, if you should pass on and enter the hereafter. Don't get me wrong, I won't be making that decision. I'm just here to gather information and relay it back to the true decision maker."

"Come on. This is ludicrous. I'm not in any coma. I've got to be dreaming. This can't be happening."

"Oh but it is happening, my friend. I'll explain more to you later." Ernest said as he turned his head and his attention to a giant banyan tree in his front yard. "Son of a bitch, that thing must be sixty feet tall now. It wasn't six when we planted it."

Though we had been standing in its shade, and the breeze was blowing even harder now, I could feel myself beginning to perspire. The wall had been a bit cool to the touch when I first put my palms on it, but now I could feel them perspiring.

"Oh yeah," I said next, "if I am in some kind of a coma, I'm sure you're just a figment of my supposed out-to-lunch subconscious. But you say no. You say you're running errands for God! Come on now, you just said 'son of a bitch.' If there is such a place as heaven, I seriously doubt they'd send an angel or whatever who talks like that."

"Pffffff," Ernest exhaled through tight lips then laughed, "Hah, hah, hah, hah! Lighten up, my friend. Up in the clouds they're not nearly as uptight as everybody down here thinks."

As much as I wanted to believe this was not happening, I was beginning to. And what Papa Hemingway said next clinched the deal.

"Okay, Jack, I just happen to know that you've done a considerable amount of reading about me. So let me ask you a few questions. I think the answers you give me just might make you a believer. Is that okay with you?"

With a tone a bit more sarcastic than I meant it to be, I said, "Sure. Go for it. Fire away."

"What is today?" he asked.

"Saturday, July second. That's why it's so crowded down here. Everybody's down for the fourth of July weekend."

"Bingo! Exactly! It's July second. What year?"

"Two-thousand-eleven," I said, now feeling like he was toying with me.

"Two-thousand-eleven, that's right. July second, two-thousand-eleven. Now, subtract fifty years from today's date. What do you come up with?"

"July second, nineteen-sixt. . . ." I froze right there, before finishing the year. "Ohhh shit! I don't believe it."

"Yes, go on Jack, finish the date."

I was stunned, and for a moment just stared at Ernest Hemingway. I really had to work hard to get the words from my mind to my tongue, but I managed.

"July second, nineteen-sixty-one. That was fifty years ago to the day. That was the day that you . . . well, you killed yourself, in Ketchum, Idaho!"

Biting his lower lip now, he slowly nodded his head as his face took on a melancholic look. I could tell his thoughts had returned to a different time and place. Probably to the hallway where he'd pulled his last trigger. I watched as his eyes glazed over.

But then he caught himself. Regrouping quickly, he deep-sixed the pensive look, cleared his throat twice then said, "That's right. Today is the fiftieth anniversary of my death. And since *you're* here in Key West, in your present condition, He thought I'd be the best man for the job. Think about it, Jack. I've been a person of interest to you for quite some time, and today is my fiftieth, so He figured what the heck, why not combine a little holiday with good old Hem's work assignment."

"Son-of-a-gun," I said slowly, "Mister Hemingway, *it is you!*"

"Ahhh, forget the mister stuff, Jack," he said waving me off. "Just call me Ernest, Papa, EH, anything you like except asshole."

He chuckled then and patted my back. "Come on now. Let's walk. Let's head down to Josie's place for a couple of cold ones. I'll fill you in on more of the details when we get there."

So I went with Ernest Miller Hemingway. I was flabbergasted. Here I was, side by side, walking up Whitehead Street with the man who single-handedly revolutionized all of modern literature.

Chapter 3

As we hoofed it toward his favorite watering hole, Ernest made no attempt to hide his disdain for what had become of the island he'd called home for ten years. All the way up Whitehead, he registered complaints such as, "What the hell has time done to this place? Look at the way they've prettied up all these houses. They've lost all their charm. And all these people. Shit, I thought it was crowded when I left for Cuba in '39. You can hardly make your way down this sidewalk anymore. And these cars . . . look at them! They're everywhere!"

But those reactions were mild. After we turned right onto Caroline and came up to busy Duval Street, he really lost it.

"Ohhhh, good mother of mercy, I can't believe my eyes! Would you look at this circus?"

"Yeah, I'll bet it has changed plenty since the 1930's, hasn't it?"

"Changed? It's a completely different place! Looks like a damn carnival. Quick, look over there, across the street—those two guys are holding hands. And get a load of all these other people. Wow. I used to think New York was crowded when I'd go to see Max Perkins at Scribner's. Hah!"

For the next minute or so Ernest said nothing. We just stood there, on the corner of Caroline and Duval as he took it all in. The expression on his old face was like that of a little boy who'd suddenly had his Christmas gifts snatched from beneath a tree.

"Back in the day," he said, "they didn't have all these funky shops either. This place looks like a miniature Shanghai, China."

"Hey, man, look to your left." I said trying to bring him back. "Check out the shirts on that man and woman coming towards us."

"Where? There must be a thousand tourists out here."

15

"Right here, Ernest." I said, swaying my eyes and throwing my head to the side. "See the couple stepping off the sidewalk—the guy with the blue tee shirt and the lady with the red tank top?"

"Well I'll be" he said, finally spotting them in the wave of humanity coming at us. "They have pictures of *me* on their shirts. Hey . . . what does that say above them?"

"Sloppy Joe's."

"Son of a gun. Looks like Josie and I have left our marks here. Wait till I tell him."

"He's up there too?"

"Yes he is. Neither of us went straight up after we died, but we both made it eventually. Come on. Let's go to the bar."

"Do you remember which way it is?"

"Do I remember which way it is? You want a slap in the back of the head, Jacky boy? Do you know how many times I've hiked up here? Hell, back in the day I could have found my way to Josie's place with my eyes closed. As a matter of fact, I can't count the times I made it home when I *was* half blind. Come on. Let's go. I'm getting thirsty."

With Ernest leading the way, we slithered and side-stepped through the onslaught of pedestrians for one more block. As we did, Ernest told me that the bricks in the wall around his house had once made up the surface of the very street we were skirting. I already knew it from my reading. His right-hand man, Toby Bruce, had gathered the bricks when work crews were tearing up Duval Street back in the thirties. I also knew that Ernest had the wall built to keep nosy tourists from gawking at his place.

"Let's sit in the back . . . at that small table," Ernest said after we pushed through the swinging doors at Sloppy Joe's. "You don't want to be at the bar, mumbling to me, with everybody watching,"

As soon as we sat down, a tall, bar-weary waitress came to our table and asked me what I wanted to drink. The name tag pinned to her floral blouse said "Desiree." Probably in her early forties, she seemed a bit old to be a Desiree.

"I'll have a Corona and a Papa Dobles." I told her.

Widening her eyes a bit she said, "Guess you're trying to make up for some lost time, eh?"

I said, "Something like that," and before she headed back to the bar, she winked at me as if she and I shared some kind of secret. It seemed odd, but I blew it off.

Out on the dance floor, a dozen loose spirits were working it out to Jimmy Buffett's "Son of a Son of a Sailor." The band was set up on a small platform, and right behind it there was a wide banner. It read "Sloppy Joe's," and there was a picture of Ernest's face on it that seemed to jump right out at the crowd. And that wasn't the only place we saw his bearded face. Everywhere we looked it was emblazoned on mugs, cups, shirts and sun visors. It was even on all the menus.

After quietly taking it all in, Ernest pointed to the wall alongside us and said, "See that sailfish hanging there?"

"Yup, I see it," I said at the exact moment our drink-toting waitress emerged from the crowd.

Snagged! I thought. *She caught me. She thinks I'm talking to myself.*

I felt like a little boy who'd been caught with his finger up his nose.

"Are you *sure* you're up to these?" she asked in a dubious tone that also had a hint of playfulness in it.

"Yeah, yeah, I'm fine. Just thinking out loud is all. Been working a bit too hard lately . . . if you know what I mean."

She gave a been-there-done-that look, put the drinks down, and then went back to work.

"Alright, Mister Hemingway," I said, as he enjoyed a belly-bouncing laugh, "Real, real funny isn't it?"

"I told you to be careful."

After looking both ways, making sure nobody was looking this time, I said "Yeah, you did."

He took a swallow of his Papa Dobles, put the glass down then leaned forward. He looked at me for a moment. Then he said, "Jack, we've had a few laughs, and that's good for both of us, but now we have to get down to business. The reason

I'm here is no laughing matter. I hate to say it, but right now, as we speak, you, my friend, are in a dire situation."

Slam! I wasn't ready for this. Suddenly I felt as if the bar's ceiling had turned black and caved in on top of me. Our carefree good time had been smothered. No longer could I hear the music or any of the excited chatter around me. It was as if I were lying beneath the ceiling's dark rubble and could only see Ernest's face. I wanted out of there. I wanted to be back out in the sunshine with all the other tourists.

"Come on, Ernest," I said, "what in the hell are you talking about . . . a dire situation?"

He raised his white brows now, dug his eyes deeper into mine and slowly said, "I am going to ask you a few questions now. At first they might sound ridiculous. But the answers you give are going to help you understand exactly what's going on. Are you ready?"

I looked at him for a moment. I studied the dead-serious expression on his face. Somehow, the scar on his forehead now seemed menacing. In a voice far less cordial than it had been, I said, "Yeah, go ahead. Ask me your questions."

"You know your name because He has allowed you to retain that much. You know who I am and certain other things. But answer me this, where do you live?"

"Come on now, what do you mean where do I live? Give me a break, Ernest. I live in . . . in . . . give me a minute. I'm just having a brain cramp."

"Are you married, Jack? If you are, what is your wife's name? Have you got any children? Where are you going to sleep tonight?"

Both my arms went limp at my sides. My knees started bouncing up and down, fast, like high-speed pistons. I cleared my throat and tried to speak but couldn't. Nothing would come out.

"I hate doing this to you, Jack, but you have to know what's going on. You don't know that you've been in an accident, do you?"

"No . . . I don't! For God's sake, Ernest, what is it? What's going on?"

"How you did it doesn't matter right now, but as we speak your body is lying in a coma, in a West Palm Beach hospital. Your skull was badly fractured. There are several tubes and a heart monitor hooked up to you. A respirator is helping you breathe."

"This whole thing is nuts. I must be dreaming. Tell me I'm dreaming."

"I can't, because you're not dreaming. You have been allotted four days with me. The information that I bring back to Him, after those four days, will determine whether you come out of that coma or . . . or you expire. The man upstairs seems to feel that your life hasn't been going in the right direction. He said he's given you a talent that you haven't put to good use."

"Wait a minute," I said waving one of those sweaty palms at him now. "Hold on. Just wait a minute here. Are you trying to tell me that the supposed all-loving God up there is going to end me just because He thinks I haven't met my *potential*? Uh, uh! I don't buy that for a minute. What is God, some kind of a production freak? He's going to end my life, because I haven't lived up to my fullest potential? Sorry, I don't believe it."

"No, Jack, you have it all wrong. He's going out of his way for you. He's considering giving you a second chance. I don't know; maybe he thinks you're a really nice guy. Maybe he likes your wife an awful lot. You do have a wife by the way, no kids, but you have a wife. And she's at your bedside as we speak."

I took a long draw from my Corona and finished it off. Then I caught the waitress's eye and held up the bottle. She nodded, and I looked back at Ernest. "I should tell her to bring back an entire tray of those Papa Dobles you like so much."

He allowed himself a slight grin, and I said, "Once again, Ernest, this doesn't seem fair."

"It's more than fair. Like everybody else in this bar, you're a mortal. He lets all of you live your own lives. He allows you to make your own decisions. And when the end comes, he rarely intercedes. Look . . . the chances of you snapping out of that coma aren't all that good. Not on your own, anyway. When I report my findings to Him, He just might decide to step in this time. He may give you that second chance."

"So in other words, *you'll* be deciding whether I live or I don't."

"Not at all, I've already told you that. I'll just be giving him my honest feedback. *He'll* be the one making the decision."

"Hmmm . . . sounds like I'm going to have to soft soap the hell out of you for the next few days, huh?"

"No, Jack. That would never work. Believe me, I'd see right through the suds."

"I know that."

Listen, why don't we just have a good time for now? I've got four days down here—you've got an opportunity—let's try to have some fun. There are places I want to take you. Places I want to revisit. I think you'll enjoy going with me."

The waitress then dropped off my cold beer. I thanked her, took a swallow then said, "Okay, Ernest, what's this supposed talent He thinks I've neglected? I can't wait to hear this one."

"Of course you won't be able to remember right now, but you've had many jobs in your life. You've done all kinds of things and never enjoyed a single one of them. Every time you mastered one thing it would soon bore you to tears. Right away, you'd be looking around for something else."

"You're right, I don't remember. But go on. I'm all ears."

"Jack, He feels the reason you've jumped around so much is because you're a very creative person. That's why you've always tired of your work so quickly. Along with your creativeness, whether you realize it or not, you're also a very insightful person. And that's why I've been sent to see you. *I* was a writer. He seems to think that you should have been one too. He believes that you still might become one, that what you're capable of putting on paper could make a difference in people's lives."

"Well, how are we going to find that out in just a few days?"

"Oh, we will! Trust me. I can already see that you communicate very well. And you ask a lot of questions. Those are good signs. But please, don't get your hopes up yet. We've got a ways to go, and I can't guarantee you anything."

Ernest then looked around the barroom. He spotted a clock then said, "You know what, it's after five. I'm getting hungry. What do you say we grab a bite?"

I agreed, downed the last of my beer then reached into my back pocket. My wallet wasn't there. The late great author laughed as he rose to his feet. Waving me off he said, "Forget it. We don't need any money. This will be taken care of."

"But what about the . . . ."

"Forget about the check, Jack. Just give the waitress a little wave on the way out."

As we walked past the bar I did give her a wave. She looked at me, smiled, and gave me another one of those knowing winks.

Once we stepped back out into the sunshine, I asked Ernest what the heck that was all about. He just said, "That? That was nothing. You haven't seen anything yet." Then he asked me, "What do you feel like eating . . . seafood?"

"Yeah, sure, that sounds good to me," I came back. "I don't imagine you know of any good restaurants down here anymore. Do you?"

"Don't worry about that. We're eating at my place."

"Your place? You mean we're going up *there to eat*?" I said, giving my head a little jerk towards the clear blue.

"Noooo!" he said with that trademark grin of his. "My place right here."

"But it's a museum now. How are we . . . ?"

With his grin widening even more, he interrupted me. Looking at me as if I were half an idiot he said, "Come on now Jack. Work with me here. Let's just go eat. I'll handle it."

21

By the time we got back to his home the place was deserted. It had closed to the public at five o'clock. Ernest fiddled for a few seconds with the locked front gate; then swung it open. The sun hadn't yet lost much of its heat, but within the confines of the brick wall, it was most comfortable. Even though the wind had died, the grounds were well shaded by its many tall trees. As we strolled up the cement walkway to the front doors, two six-toed cats, one black and the other a dark gray, scooted by in front of us. Ernest said, "I wonder where the hell they all came from. The only animals we ever had when I lived here were peacocks."

Although I was both honored and thrilled to be going into Ernest's home with "The Man" himself, there was a funereal feel to the experience. For the most part, I'd had a good time with him that afternoon, but the dark side of our encounter hadn't left the edges of my consciousness. I, Jack Phelan, could very well be on my way out. Don't get me wrong, my mind wasn't a whirlwind of fear. I was not paralyzed by the terrified feeling most people get when death's cold, dark fingers suddenly reach out for them. I wasn't my usual self. I was cognizant, but then again I really wasn't. I truly didn't know who I was, nor did I have any idea who or what I'd be leaving behind.

Sure, I definitely wanted to live, but if the call came from above, I'd have nothing to grieve. It certainly bothered me that I'd leave behind the wife Ernest told me was at my bedside. From what he'd said, I was pretty sure she would mourn my loss and suffer much heartache. But then again, I had absolutely no idea who she was, nor even who I was.

Chapter 4

When we stepped inside the house, Ernest froze. Standing tall as his old frame would allow, I could tell he was struggling to remain strong. I watched his face closely while he surveyed the room. As if in great pain, his eyes pulled tight, and his white beard started to quiver. I leaned toward him and gently patted his back.

"Ernest, do you need some time alone? I can wait outside for a while."

"No, that's alright. But I want to go upstairs for a few minutes . . . alone, if you don't mind. It's been quite some time since I've been here, and this isn't going to be easy. Maybe you can just wait down here."

"Sure." I said. "You bet."

Inquisitive as I was, I didn't poke around. I sat on the sofa and listened to Ernest's slow, heavy footsteps on the floor above. They moved from room to room. Every time they stopped, I figured he was looking at some kind of memento, maybe an old framed photograph; a mounted fish, or the blood pressure readings he used to scribble on the bathroom wall each day. I couldn't be sure. But when I heard the squeak of old bed springs, I knew he had lain down.

A few minutes passed, and I heard him get back up. He only took a few steps before stopping. Then I heard another sound—a very distinct sound. It was the tapping of typewriter keys. There were exactly seven taps—each of them slowly spaced—as if Ernest Hemingway had typed "The End" to one of his stories. After that I heard sobs. They were muted, and they were low, but I know I heard sobs coming from the second floor of the Hemingway house.

Only a minute or two after the sobbing stopped, Ernest came back down the stairs. I was surprised at how quickly he descended the steps after such a heart-wrenching experience. But what really got to me was his appearance. Other than his white hair being a bit tousled, he looked invigorated. It was as if he had just woken from a restful night's sleep to a long-awaited day. But I knew his sudden vitality had nothing to do with rest. It was fueled by an immense sense of relief. Ernest Hemingway had faced up to something he'd dreaded for a long, long time.

"Okay, Jack, ready to eat?" he asked.

"Sure, whenever you are." I said, as I got up from the sofa.

"Come on. Let's go out by the pool."

I followed him thinking he must have decided to barbeque the seafood he'd talked about. But as he stepped out the side door leading to the patio and pool he said, "Hot damn! Can you smell that?"

"You bet. It smells like a seafood smorgasbord."

And it was. Opposite each other, on a round table out there, were two place settings lying atop straw mats. There were plates, bowls, gleaming knives, forks, and spoons, along with green linen napkins, and matching stemmed glasses full of white wine. Between the settings and two tall bottles of wine there was a platter of piping hot seafood that could have fed four hungry men. It was heaped high with slabs of golden-fried mahi-mahi, fresh jumbo shrimp, scallops, and onion rings. Alongside it was a kettle of conch chowder, a bowl of salad and oven toasted bread.

Wasting no time in relieving the platter from some of its weight, I said, "Man, does this look good." I then squeezed a couple of slices of fresh lemon over my loaded plate, picked up a shrimp and dipped it into red sauce. It tasted as if it had come straight from the ocean into the pan. And it probably had.

"Ohhh," I said, "this is to kill for. I feel like I've died and gone to heaven."

"Don't be rushing it, Jacky boy; you may not be quite ready for the clouds yet."

We shared a quick chuckle, toasted to my uncertain future then went to work on the seafood.

When we finally finished more than we should have, we moved the show to the side of the swimming pool. Both of us armed with a bottle and a glass, we lowered ourselves into two rattan lounge chairs facing the water. Without saying a thing, we took in the surroundings.

By now most of the sunset revelers at Mallory Square had surely retreated to their homes, hotel rooms, or the bars of Duval Street. A thin, pale slice of moon had made its first appearance, and the trees above us had lost their color. Two cats scouted around a dark bush, and a couple of nearby dogs exchanged barks. The crickets had made their presence known, and a car drove by on the other side of the wall.

"It's not easy coming back here, is it Ernest?"

He took a sip of wine, looked at me for a moment then said, "Yes and no. I always believed that life was a one-shot deal. That's why, when I was alive, I always tried to get the very most out of it. I had a damn good time, and there wasn't much I was sorry for. But being back here now . . . well, let's just say my perspective has changed a little. And a few regrets that have been asleep in my mind for a long, long time have been jarred awake."

"I don't suppose you care to talk about them."

"Not really, Jack, but thanks. None of it matters anymore. A man can learn from his past mistakes, and he should, but reliving them . . . that does absolutely no good. If you rehash all the poor choices and decisions you've made, it's like stabbing yourself again and again. Your spirit will always carry its deepest scars. There's no way to eliminate them. And from time to time, they'll come out of hiding on their own. When they do, let them reprimand you. Take what's coming; ride it out, get it over with. But by all means, don't ever entertain them any longer than you have to, and never invite them back."

"That makes nothing but sense. Well put."

"That was what I was doing upstairs when we first got here. I took what came at me. I reacted then did the best I could to let it go."

Ernest had been looking up at the stars when he'd made that last point. Now he returned to earth and looked me square in the eyes.

"Keep that advice up here," he said, tapping his head. "You can't remember your life or your personal relationships right now. Oh sure, you recall some things like reading about me, shrimp, fish, wine, certain songs and such, but that's only because He's allowing you to. In three more days, all the rest of it will come back to you. Whether you remain down here or you go to another world, your memories *will return.* Just don't let them eat at you. Take whatever comes then move forward the best you can. Comprende, amigo?"

"I'll do the best I can, Ernest. I just hope that's good enough."

"Ah, come on," he said, straightening up now, giving me a slap on the knee. "It's been a long day for both of us. What do you say we go inside? With all I've got planned for tomorrow, you're going to need a good night's rest."

"What have you got planned?" I asked as I pushed myself up from the chair.

"Forget it, Jack. If I told you where we were going and who you were going to meet you'd never believe me. But I can guarantee this . . . you, my friend, are in for the time of your life."

Chapter 5

I don't know where in the house Ernest slept that night nor if he slept at all. But because he offered to let me crash in the master bedroom, I had a sneaking suspicion that messengers from the clouds didn't require any sleep.

The second floor bedroom was situated in a back corner of the Spanish Colonial house. Like all the other rooms it had high ceilings and dark wood floors. It seemed very odd to me that instead of a ceiling fan above the bed, there was a large chandelier. But that really didn't matter. I slept with all the windows wide open, as well as the two doors leading out to the veranda. And boy, did I sleep.

As soon as I hit that mattress, I was out like a KO'd boxer. And it's a good thing because before I knew it, I heard Ernest's voice again. I couldn't see him because it was still dark as a moonless midnight, but I heard him standing over me.

"Wake up, Jack. Come on. You can't sleep your life away. Heh, heh, heh! Whoops, sorry about that. I couldn't resist."

"Very funny, Ernest. What the hell time is it?"

"It's about four-thirty."

"Four-thirty! Are you kidding me? Come on, let me go back to sleep."

"Forget about the time. Hurry up and get dressed. Breakfast is ready, and you and I are going on a little trip."

"Yeah, yeah, alright . . . just give me a few minutes. I'll be right down."

"Okay. And don't worry about making the bed or anything. All that will be taken care of."

"Somehow that doesn't surprise me," I said as Ernest stepped out of the dark room.

"I'm glad of that," he shot back as he started high-tailing it down the stairs like an excited kid, "because you ain't seen nuthin' yet, kiddo. Ha, ha, ha, ha!"

As much as I didn't want to, I then reached over and turned on the bedside lamp. I squinted at the nightstand where I'd piled my clothes the night before. Then I squinted even more, and it had nothing to do with the intrusive light. My clothes had disappeared. In their place was a neatly folded change of clothes. There were clean skivvies, a pair of Hemingwayesque khaki Bermudas, and a beige light-weight safari shirt. I couldn't believe it. But the real kicker came when I slung my legs off the bed to stand up. Feeling something beneath my feet, I spread them open and there was a brand spanking new pair of size-eleven deck shoes.

Ernest and I hardly talked during breakfast. We were too busy working over a tall stack of pancakes drenched in hot syrup. We didn't need to talk. We were getting along just fine.

When we finally sat back in our chairs at the long dining room table, our bellies full, slurping the last of our coffee, I said, "Okay, Ernest, what's the surprise? What do you have planned for today?"

"Are you all done?"

"Yeah, I'm good to go."

"Then let's take off. I want to show you rather than tell you."

Dressed in clean, roped-up shorts and a white Guaynabo, Ernest rose from the table. Rolling his sleeves up to his elbows, he said, "Get that cooler on the counter over there . . . it's full of sandwiches, fruit, beer, water and ice. It's somewhat heavy, but we're just going a few blocks. I'll get the thermos of coffee."

When we stepped out of the house into the darkness, all was quiet. The sky was clear, and the sliver of a moon had migrated across it. We trekked up the wide concrete walkway, and before locking the gate behind, Ernest turned and took one final look at his house. After standing there for a moment with the Thermos dangling from his hand, he said, "They were good years here in Key West. Damn good years." Then there was more silence.

It was as if he were looking at a close friend in a casket for the last time. I knew he was dealing with memories—waiting for them to pass—waiting for their nostalgic hurt to wear off. When we finally did walk away, neither of us said a word. All that could be heard was our footsteps on the sidewalk as we coursed the brick wall out front. And there was more of the same as we continued past long, darkened rows of conch houses.

As we walked on in silence, I thought about the man alongside me. Although I had just hooked up with him the day before, I'd not only witnessed some of his emotional displays, but I'd felt them as well. To say I was surprised by his heartfelt actions would be a huge understatement. After all, Ernest Hemingway—the man, the myth, the legend he'd become—had been forged from more than just his literary accomplishments. He was supposed to have been a hard man, with thick skin and calluses on his knuckles and heart. But I already knew differently. That was not the Ernest Hemingway I was walking with in the pre-dawn darkness. This man had neither a stainless steel persona nor heart.

The cooler I'd been lugging was now getting heavier with each step. The muscles in my arms had stretched to new lengths. As we crossed yet another street, I was just about to tell Ernest that I needed to put it down, but I didn't. There were docks and black water before us. In the darkness I could just make out about a half dozen boats. We were close enough now to hear the gentle slap of water on their hulls.

"Looky there, Jack," Ernest said, as we stepped onto the wooden platform, "third one down . . . on the right."

Still in a predawn half-trance, I could not believe my eyes. Tied to the dock just up ahead, her cabin gently lit by a single light bulb, was the Pilar.

I turned to Ernest alongside me and said, "Come on . . . get out of here! It can't be."

He said nothing, but there was a smile across his face as wide as the yacht's beam. Unable to hold back his excitement any longer, he sped up in that rolling gait of his. With heavy heels plunking the wooden planks, Hem moved with the renewed energy of an old man being reunited with something he had loved deeply for a long, long time.

The closer I got, the more magnificent his thirty-eight-foot fishing boat looked. With her low gunwales, she seemed to straddle the water rather than float upon it. Faint light from the bare bulb atop a piling mirrored off her freshly-painted, black hull, and the wooden cabin shone as if the varnish had not yet dried. The Pilar looked brand new—like she must have looked in 1934 when her maiden voyage took her from Brooklyn's Wheeler Shipyard to a waiting Ernest in Miami.

By the time I reached the boat, Ernest was already on the wide, green deck near the stern. He was checking out the ladder-back fighting chair—swiveling and sliding it—as if preparing once again to do battle with the finned Goliaths of the South Seas.

"Oh," he finally said. "Sorry . . . here, give me the cooler."

I swung it over the transom to him; then I climbed aboard. She was like something out of a museum and in all reality was. For the fifty years since Ernest's death, Pilar had been dry-docked alongside his Cuban home. Recently it had been restored along with the house which was now open to the public.

As Ernest kicked over the seventy-five horsepower Chrysler engine, I heard him say in a gentle tone, "That a girl. Papa's taking you home."

She purred in the darkness like a reliable friend. With her gurgling prop and the low rumble of the exhaust, it was as if Pilar were telling us she was raring to go. Feeling the engine's powerful vibration beneath my feet, I poked around the deck until the skipper, without looking over his shoulder, said, "Come on, Jack, untie the lines. We're going to Cuba."

It wasn't long before the first pale gray light of a new day appeared on the port side. Standing alongside Ernest at the helm, I opened the Thermos and poured a steamy cup of coffee. I offered it to Hem, but he waved me off. Looking around as I took a sip, I thought how nothing on earth offers as much hope as daybreak on the ocean. Then I turned to watch the boat's wake spreading behind us. The lights of Key West were quickly drowning in the ocean behind us.

"Cuba's about ninety miles, right Ernest?"

"That's a positive. We should reach Cojimar in about six hours. Once we get there, it's only a ten minute taxi ride to Havana."

"So we're going to Havana?"

"We'll be spending the night at my old place, the Finca Vigia, but we're going to Havana first."

"What are we going to do in Havana?" I asked, taking another sip of the strong coffee.

"That's going to be another surprise, Jack. But I'll tell you this much, we're going to the Floridita Bar. We have to meet somebody there."

"Somebody I know?"

"You know *of* him, but that's it. I'm not going to tell you anymore. But don't worry, I guarantee we'll have a good time."

"Sounds good to me."

"Hey," Ernest then blurted, pointing through the now open windshield, "look there . . . just to the left."

We were well in the Gulf Stream by now, and a sailfish was quickly closing on a hapless ballyhoo. The rising sun had colored the water pink, and the sailfish cut through the surreal surface like a heat-seeking torpedo. Spending more time out of the water than in it, the frantic skittering baitfish changed directions twice, but it didn't have a chance. The sail closed in; its beak rose from the water as it opened its mouth. Then smash! The water erupted with a showery explosion, and pink, sunlit droplets splayed in every direction. It was the kind of vision that remains stamped in a fisherman's mind till the day of his very last cast.

"How about some of that coffee?" Ernest asked, his eyes still fixed on the rippling water.

"Sure. Sorry. I didn't know if . . . ."

"That's fine. There's another cup in that cabinet— beneath the counter in front of you."

As I handed Ernest the coffee in an old metal cup, his eyes were squinting in the new sunshine. "You know, Jack," he said, "Mother Nature is a chameleon. Sometimes, when she shows her beautiful side, her kindness and generosity can be limitless. Other times, forget it; she can be one heartless, malevolent whore."

"I think I know exactly what you mean."

He reached for a green visor hanging next to him on the cabin wall. Letting go of the wheel for a moment as he slid the visor onto his head and adjusted it, he said, "Have you ever seen a lion take down a zebra? How about a pack of coyotes finishing off a fawn, or a shark rip apart a hooked marlin? It's all about survival. But wow, it can be incredibly cruel."

"Have you ever asked Him about that? Why things couldn't have been set up differently?"

"No, but you know what . . . I will."

I thought about what he'd just said for a moment. Then, knowing that Ernest had ended thousands of lives with his guns and fishing rods, I asked him something against my better judgment.

"I've never been a hunter, Ernest, although I too love to fish. You've been both. Have you ever regretted taking the lives of so many animals?"

Instantly I was sorry I'd asked him that.

Still looking at me, his eyes narrowed. Beneath the visor I saw his forehead all scrunched up. Had I not known the real Ernest Hemingway, I'd have thought he just might be getting ready to let go of the wheel and nail me with a hard right.

After a short eternity, he'd finally turned away. His gaze returned to the wide, watery horizon beyond the bow, and the angry expression on his face evolved into something else. His stormy look lost its ferociousness. The undulating muscles protruding from his jaw were no longer flexing. The initial impact of my question was waning. I couldn't tell if he was going to ignore my question about killing animals or if he was hunting for just the right words to answer it. Either way I wished I could take it back.

Still looking straight ahead, he held the metal cup in my direction and said, "Would you give me one more small splash, Jack?"

"Sure. You bet."

I poured a bit from the thermos and handed it back. He took a sip, rested the cup on the counter behind the wheel, and said, "No, I don't regret what I've done. I loved what I was doing. Considering who I was at the time, hunting and fishing were perfectly fine. It was the right thing to do, fulfill my deepest passions. But I'll grant you this . . . you did hit a sore spot."

I looked down. Then like a small boy who was sorry for something he shouldn't have done, I said in a low tone, "I had no right asking . . . ."

"Forget it. Don't let it eat at you, Jack. It was a perfectly legitimate question. It stung like a mean-assed wasp, but it was legitimate. As a matter of fact, it was a good sign. A writer must ask the tough questions. It's the only way to get to the heart of the truth."

"Well, I'm still not too happy," I said, lifting my head to the windshield just in time to see a flying fish skitter across the water's indigo surface. The sun was higher now, allowing the water to take back its natural color. We'd been running for close to an hour, and the Gulf Stream beneath us was very deep—deep as the feelings that Ernest was about to express.

"Fish," he said, nodding to where the flying fish had just ended its flight, "I don't mind killing fish. Sure, just as I have written, when you've battled a big one for a long time—he on one end of the line, you on the other, you can't help but to feel connected to him by more than just the line. You respect that fish, and he respects you. It's a personal thing, and the longer the fight goes on the more you respect each other. The crew and your friends—they can be right alongside the chair with you, but it's still just you and that fish. You can actually grow to love a giant marlin, tuna, or swordfish. And as much as you want to get the gaff into him, once you've caught many big fish, you begin to feel somewhat sentimental about ending such a magnificent animal's life. Smaller fish . . . I still don't much care. As long as you're going to put it to some kind of use, that's fine. Remember, Jack, the nervous system of a fish is not all that well developed, and it's not a very deep thinker. Sure a fish can be wary. It can be anxious. It can fight. It can kill. But it's all about instincts, not about thinking things out. They don't have that capability."

Lifting one gnarled finger from the wheel now, pointing it to the two o'clock position, he then said, "See it on the horizon, Jack?"

"No . . . I don't see anything."

"Look harder. It's a boat coming our way, a ship, either a freighter or an ocean liner. This is one of the busiest shipping lanes there is. I'm surprised we haven't seen anything up till now."

"Ohhh yeah, I see it. But it's barely a speck."

"You spend the time out here I've spent you can tell what it is. They won't reach us for a good twenty minutes. Anyway, getting back to what we were talking about—killing animals, mammals. Am I sorry about killing them? Let's just say that near the end of my life, just before they ruined me with those frigging electro-shock treatments, I did get to the point where I preferred watching a majestic animal rather than taking it down."

"Kind of like the old hunter thing, huh?"

"Exactly like the old hunter thing."

"I never dreamed that 'The' Ernest Hemingway would ever feel that way."

"Hahhh," he laughed, "a lot of people back in the day, as well as today, would be damn surprised at how old Papa feels about a lot of things."

"Knowing you like I do after just a short time, I'm sure people would be stunned."

"Well, thanks friend," he said looking at me over the rim of the eyeglasses he'd put on a few minutes earlier. "What did you think of me before we met?"

"Oh hell, I don't know how to answer that."

"Malarky! Now spill it Twinster."

"Twinster? What's this Twinster stuff?"

Looking at my forehead now, nodding at it, he said, "Once that nasty gash heals, you're going to have a damned good scar. Whether you go cloud dancing, stay down here or whatever, it's going to look an awful lot mine," he said, tapping his twice. "That's why I called you Twinster."

"Hey," I blurted then, "you know something? That ship, it's getting closer now. And it seems to be heading right for us."

"We have plenty of time to . . . ," then he stopped right there. Something was weird. He acted as if he suddenly had a premonition or a revelation.

"Son of a gun! You know what, Jack? I just realized something. We have plenty of time to get out of this cruise ship's way, but whoever's running it can't see us. Nobody can!"

"What are you talking about, they can't see us?"

"*Come on man!* Think about it. Is He going to let the world see the Pilar back out on the ocean?"

"I'll be damned. Of course not. That's freaking amazing, but how does He . . . ?"

"It's called supreme visual deception. I heard about it upstairs. He can put anything he wants down here, could be a mountain big as Kilimanjaro, if He doesn't want it to be seen, it isn't. Amen. Done deal."

Shaking his head in awe, a small ironic smile on his lips, Ernest turned the wheel to the port side.

Over the course of the next two hours, we saw a few yachts and freighters, another cruise ship, and one long yellow Cigarette boat that was hell-bent on going airborne. We also saw more flying fish and a school of bonito that had churned three acres of the ocean's surface into a white froth.

Even though we'd been standing in the shade of the cockpit the whole time, it felt like we were in the doldrums. I don't know how high the temperature got, but it was oppressively hot. And it was humid. It felt like a steamed-up locker room out there in all that sunny stillness. I was sweating profusely, but for some reason, a Godly one I supposed, my partner's shirt was still dry as could be.

"Ernest," I said, as a droplet fell from my eyebrow, "would you mind if I went below? I'd like to lie down for a while. We got up awfully early this morning, and this heat is . . ."

"Sure, go ahead. But you'd better drink some of that water first. It's in the cooler."

I fished a cold plastic bottle out of the ice, took two long swallows then went down below.

As I stepped into Pilar's dark cabin, it felt as if I were entering a cabin of a different sort. With its close wooden walls and ceiling, it seemed like a small, isolated North Woods cabin. Like a place where you might find a silent monk down on his knees. The seagoing quarters of the late great Ernest Hemingway not only had that ambience, it also seemed every bit as hallowed. But there was something else in the belly of the Pilar. Something I don't think you'd find in a monk's humble cabin. There were ghosts. Not only could I feel them, but I could see them as well.

Chapter 6

Inside that quiet cabin I first saw one of Hem's long gone writer friends. John Dos Passos, the illegitimate socialist son of an industrialist supporter, was sitting with his wife, Katy, on a green sofa. They each had a drink in hand and both looked very happy. I saw a young Ernest sitting at a small desk down there. He was scribbling notes about a battle he had recently fought from his deck-mounted fighting chair. I could see members of his "mob" and the Pilar's crew crowded in the cabin. They were toasting drinks to another successful day's fishing. Then I noticed that Ernest had moved. He was now sitting, smiling, and joking with his last three wives at the small dining table. Then, up ahead, I heard something else. Sounds were coming from beyond an open doorway leading to the sleeping quarters. They were moans.

All at once a faint chorus of pleasurable female moans wafted into the room. It filled the air and lingered like a soft, satisfied hum. For some reason none of the other guests seemed to notice.

Not believing my ears, I smacked the side of my head a few times. It wasn't until I started walking toward the portal that the gentle choir grew fainter. When I stepped into the miniature bedroom, the sound ceased completely. Just like that, there was silence again. But as I stood between the two small beds, there was something else in the air—something every bit as unnerving as what I'd just heard. It was a smell, a scent. Permeating the eerie silence was a combination of fragrances—a sweet, subtle mélange of many different perfumes.

Whoosh, I thought, *I'd better get some sleep. This heat's getting to me more than I realized.*

I took one last gulp from the water I'd been carrying and put the empty bottle on a table; then I lay down on one of the bunks. The bed was not very long. I had to jackknife my legs at the knees to fit on it. But that didn't matter. After only a few minutes of trying to decide whether or not I was losing my head or what I had just witnessed had in fact been real, I fell into a dreamy state of unconsciousness. Then my subconscious took over. And that mysterious, uncontrollable part of the human mind started sending me messages.

I dreamed of an incredibly beautiful lady. She was the type of woman who made men howl in the privacy of their own secret dreams. Long, thick, auburn hair streamed down both sides of her fresh-cream face, and her exotic emerald eyes held me a willing prisoner. She had a rare strain of beauty that not only tortures men with desire but overwhelms them with an unexplainable jealousy as well—a jealousy rooted in the realization that she belongs to someone else and cannot be theirs. Though she was a bit on the tall side, she moved like a ballerina. As she approached me, her every move was gilded with grace.

I was lying flat on my back in a hospital bed, and it was pretty dark in the room. The heart monitor alongside the bed only beeped once every two seconds. Its digits and graph glowed green. A respirator helped me breathe, and all kinds of tubes and needles were shoved and poked into me.

Even had my eyes been open, I'd have barely seen the woman in the faint green glow of the machine. But I could see her in my dream, striding toward me in black heels, snug jeans, and a man-tailored shirt that she filled out like no man on earth could.

She sat alongside me on the narrow bed. And with her face tinged in green, she gently stroked my hair back. As she lovingly slid a hand over my head, careful not to touch my bandaged gash, there were tears glistening in her eyes.

"Jack," she said, "come back honey. Don't you dare leave me; we have far too many memories to make yet."

This woman in my dream seemed so familiar. I knew her face, her body, her walk, her gestures and her voice. Somehow, I knew I loved her. I didn't know why because I couldn't place her. And that hurt deeply. I felt as empty as a long-dead, hollow tree. I ached to hear her speak again. I needed to hear more. Finally, she drew a deep breath and prepared to speak.

But she didn't. She ran out of time because I was literally bounced right out of my dream. There was a thunderous thud. The entire top half of my body lifted high off the mattress and then slammed back onto it. It felt like the Pilar had fallen off the roof of a three story building. The hull beneath the bunk crashed on the water as if it were concrete. My entire body jarred. And when I awoke, I immediately realized how lucky I'd been to land back on the padded mattress.

Then the bow rose again. It lifted so high it seemed we were about to go airborne.

"Ernest! Ernest!" I hollered as I fought my way into the adjoining cabin, heading for the doorway.

All the guests were gone, and the floor there was soaked with water. Spanning my arms out like wings, trying to prevent myself from slamming into a wall or anything else, I sloshed my way toward the exit. I looked like an inexperienced daredevil walking a high wire as the bow lifted higher, and the thirty-eight foot hull rocked and rolled. I knew she was about to crash down again.

With my sneakers, socks and the bottoms of my pant legs now soaked, I opened the door to the deck. More water, gallons and gallons of it, rushed in.

The wind was howling louder than I'd ever heard it before. But with Ernest standing right there at the helm, I was able to hear his desperate voice. "Close that door, quick! The cabin's going to fill up with this damn water!"

By the time I managed to close it behind me, two full beer cans had washed below with the deluge of water. The cooler, upended on the deck, was lying open in a foot of water. Obviously, when I was down below and the boat slammed hard down, a monster wave had washed over the bow and cockpit. I didn't know which was louder, that wind or the deafening torrents of rain pounding away at the ocean's surface.

With the sky now as black as a midnight eclipse, I shouted to Ernest, "My good God, what's happening out here?"

"The Bermuda Triangle! We're in it! Never saw anything like this in my life! Here, quick, get this on," he yelled, flinging an orange lifejacket at me. "Don't bother buckling it! Just slip it on. We're dropping over the edge of this gargantuan wave right now, and the boat's heavy as a pack of pregnant elephants!"

I couldn't see the wave before us, but just like Ernest, I felt the bow begin to drop. Down, down, down, into the hellacious blackness we plunged. It seemed like forever as we waited for the impact. The Pilar was nosing almost straight down, like a hell-bound kamikaze.

"I don't know why He's doing this!" Ernest hollered, his thin hair lifting in the tremendous wind.

Then we hit the trough. There was a BOOM! The concussion was bone-rattling.

It felt like we were in a ten-ton runaway elevator that had crashed at the bottom of a death-black shaft. My legs were about to buckle from the tremendous force. They didn't, but the boat then listed hard to the right. I couldn't hold on any longer.

As I flew into the cockpit wall, I swore I heard Lucifer's demonic laugh. Ernest somehow managed to hold onto the wheel, but his legs swung from beneath him and slammed into the cabin door. He howled in pain, and since he hadn't let go of the wheel, the boat jerked even more sharply to the side, and it swayed even more dangerously. I thought every plank and board in the hull would explode into splinters. The vessel jounced very, very hard, and it shuddered as if terrified. Up against the wall like I was, I heard and felt the wood creaking and straining.

Ernest had pulled himself back to his feet and was giving it all he had at the helm. Dark as it was, I was close enough to see him as he fought to gain control. His face and eyes were so intent you'd have thought the old man was fighting for his own life. But he wasn't. He was already set for all eternity. He had his place in the hereafter. No, Ernest Hemingway was not fighting for himself. He was trying to save both me and his beloved Pilar from certain disaster.

Angry thunder grumbled loud overhead, and the whole boat trembled again. Then a bolt of bright lightning flashed so close that the electricity raised the wet hair on my neck and arms. It's short, erratic light lit up Ernest's rugged old face for just a split second. And as I looked at his white hair, beard, wrinkles, and scars, I suddenly felt a deep love for this man. And I suddenly believed he'd somehow get us out of this mess. But before he could, something very strange happened. I witnessed a miracle.

And as I watched, I knew it had to be divine intervention. Through the boat's windshield, Ernest and I both saw a pinhole of white light suddenly appear in the bible-black sky. Neither of us could believe our eyes when a lone thin beam, as if from a heavenly spotlight, pushed closer and closer until it shone on the bow in front of us. And at that exact moment, all the malevolent clouds that had enveloped the entire sky began to lift. It was the weirdest thing I'd ever seen.

For three-hundred-and-sixty-degrees around the Pilar, the doomsday overcast began to lift from the horizon. At first there was but a tiny sliver of bright blue everywhere the sky met the ocean. Then, as if somebody or something in the heavens were hauling up a monstrous, evil net, the clouds rose from the edge of the sea like an upside-down tornado. The higher the net's bottom rose, the more the seas settled down. The rain suddenly subsided; the sunlight brightened, and more and more blue sky appeared. It was as if this amazing phenomenon had been choreographed. The higher the ugly clouds lifted, the bluer the ocean's surface became.

Then it was over.

The heat was no longer oppressive. The trade winds had picked up, the ocean calmed down, and there was just a ruffle on its surface. Ernest and I reopened the foldout windshield so we could feel the breeze. Still holding the wheel, the skipper turned toward the stern, and I followed suit.

The flooded deck was draining back into the sea. The water that was left was littered with soggy sandwiches, seaweed, a few full beer cans, two water bottles, and a single orange starfish.

As he assessed the battle scene, Ernest said, "It was a test, Jack. I've not communicated with Him, but I *know* it was a test. Not for me, because I'm already gone, but for you."

He pushed his hair back, picked his drenched sun visor up from the floor, pulled it over his forehead and said, "Do me a favor. Grab me one of those beers. I don't give a shit if they're piss-warm. Give me a beer."

I retrieved two and popped them both open.

As I handed one to Ernest, he turned back toward the windshield. He squinted then said, "I think I see the coast. We should be docking in Cojimar within the hour."

Chapter 7

When we reached the shallows along the Cuban coastline, Ernest pointed to a beige stingray skittering along the sandy bottom. A moment later I spotted a seemingly motionless barracuda suspended in the gin-clear water. It wasn't in the mood for company, and with one quick swipe of its tail, it zoomed out of sight. We were a hundred yards from the now dilapidated pier where Papa had tied up Pilar for twenty years. As we eased closer, three dark-skinned boys in cutoff shorts dove from what was left of the concrete structure into the warm Caribbean water.

"Look at that," Ernest said in a surprised and happy tone. "Cojimar doesn't look all that different than it used to."

"How many years has it been?"

"Over fifty. I left here in 1960. Hey, look over there," he said pointing to something just beyond the seawall before us, "in the middle of that circle of pillars. It's a bust . . . of me. See it? It's looking right at us. I'll be a son of a gun."

"Yeah, I've seen pictures of it in books. I read that after you died your fishermen friends went around collecting old propellers, anchors, things like that. They melted them down so they could have a tribute to you made. I think that was around '62."

"I'll bet my old skipper Gregorio Fuentes was behind that."

"He must have had something to do with it because I've seen a picture of him and some other fishermen standing in front of it."

Ernest paused, nodding his head while he studied the bust. Then he looked back toward the dock. "Looks like those kids have cleared out of the way. Let's pull her in."

"The middle of the dock has collapsed," I said. "How are we going to get to shore, swim?"

"Hell, Jack, we're already drenched," he said with a chuckle. Then turning to me, looking like he knew something

I didn't, he added, "I've got a funny feeling we'll get over there without swimming."

A minute or two later I found out he was right. After climbing out of the Pilar and tying her lines to the narrow dock, I peeked over the other side of it. A small rowboat with two oars just happened to be waiting there.

"This just gets better and better," I said as Ernest stepped from the gunwales onto the concrete beside me.

"Oh yeah? Take a look at what's waiting for us over there," he said, jutting his head toward the shoreline.

A yellow 1953 Chevrolet was parked there. The black letters on its side read Havana Taxi.

"Come on. Let's get into this teacup and row over there. I'd love to hang around a while, stop into La Terraza for a drink, but like I said, we've got to meet somebody in Havana."

During the cab ride to Havana, Ernest and I didn't exchange a single word. The old taxi driver with dried-leather skin and tight gray rings for hair would have surely heard us talking. With seemingly nobody but me in the back seat, he'd have thought I was loco. He'd probably have gunned the ancient Chevy to the nearest loony bin rather than the El Floridita bar. Who knows? He might also have signed himself in after hearing two different voices coming from just one crazy gringo turista.

As we motored through the streets of Old Havana, Ernest did tap me on the shoulder a few times. Although some of the grand old buildings had been restored, many in the area were in a state of ill repair. Each time he spotted an exceptionally decrepit one, he'd shake his head and point toward it. Then he'd look back at me with a mournful look as if asking, what the hell has happened here?

But the taxi ride was short. And before I knew it, the driver was braking in front of the El Floridita on Monserrate Street. I didn't know what to do when the little man looked over his shoulder at me as if he expected to be paid.

Uh oh, I thought, *doesn't he know about the divine plan? I don't have a dime in my pocket. What's next?*

Not knowing what else to do, I gave him a wink as if to say, *You know what's going down here*. He just narrowed his eyes and said something in Spanish that I didn't understand.

Just as I was thinking, *Oh shit, he doesn't have a clue*, the curbside door next to Ernest opened up. Here I was three feet away from it when my invisible friend opens it and steps out. With surprising speed, the driver jerked his eyes toward the door then back at me. They were no longer narrowed. They were now wide as barroom coasters.

"Vamos! Vamos!" he began to shout as if I were some kind of voodoo prince. Quickly, I slid across the seat toward the open door. In one well-practiced motion—faster than the speed of light—he made the sign of the cross and started babbling away. I couldn't understand his words, but I darn well knew that he was praying. I sprung out of that cab, and the instant I closed the door, he peeled out of there like he'd come out of an Indie 500 pit stop.

As he sped down Monseratte Street, Ernest and I just stood on the sidewalk cracking up. Because I appeared to be standing there alone popping a gut all by myself, I was on the receiving end of more than a few strange looks from the people walking by. But I couldn't help it. The poor cab driver was frantic. He was zipping around cars on that narrow cobblestone street like a desperate, dying sinner with but five minutes to find a confessional booth.

After we calmed down some, I followed Ernest through the El Floridita's front door. He lumbered right over to the hallowed corner of the bar where on countless nights he had presided over the rich, the famous, and the not so famous. Here it was half a century after his demise, and his stool was still reserved in his honor. For years, absolutely nobody had been allowed to sit there. But what was really strange on this day was that packed as the bar was, two deep in places, the stools on both sides of Ernest's were also vacant. I couldn't help but to think there had been yet another divine intervention.

As Ernest sat on his and I climbed on the one to his left, he looked beyond me then jutted his head. "Would you look at this? I'll be a son of a gun . . . it's a statue of me."

I couldn't miss the full-size, bronze Ernest. He seemed to be standing sentinel—watching intently all that was going on before him. With his back to the wall, with one foot on the railing, and with an elbow on the wooden bar top, there was an unfriendly look on his face. He appeared to be challenging somebody—staring them down.

"Wow, Ernest," I said, still gazing at the statue, "somebody did one heck of a job with that!"

The tourist couple alongside me stopped their conversation. After giving each other a funny look, they stared at me from the corners of their eyes.

"Oh . . . excuse me. Sorry. Just thinking out loud is all."

Then I turned back to the real Ernest and heard him chortle.

"Okay, mister hotshot," I whispered, "real funny."

He good-naturedly waved me off, and then I checked out the surroundings. "You know, this is a pretty nice place. Look at the high ceilings and fancy settings on all the tables. And these bartenders, they all wear red jackets. A regular guy like me isn't used to this . . . ."

"How do you know who you are?"

"C'mon, you know what I mean. Look how I'm dressed. Not only that, but just a couple of hours ago I was fighting for my life in some freak Bermuda Triangle phenomenon. I must really be a sight."

"Ahhh, don't worry about it. Just run your fingers through your hair a couple of times."

I felt the back pocket of my shorts. There was a comb there—a brand new one.

"Well looky here," I said holding it up for Ernest to see, "I just *happen* to have a comb."

Then when I started scanning the spacious restaurant for the men's room, Ernest said, "It's right back there. You might think about slapping a little water on your face, too. You are looking a little crusty and salty."

"Cute, Papa! Real cute! I'll be right back."

As I made my way past all the mid-afternoon patrons, I could tell they were mostly tourists. All the way down the long side of the bar, people were engaged in spirited conversations with hands waving and gesturing. Most of the excited chatter was in English, and I thought I picked up more than a few Canadian accents. In the adjoining dining area, all but two of the linen-covered tables were empty. But when I walked by one occupied by a family of four, the delicious aroma of steamed tamales and black bean soup reminded me that I hadn't eaten since breakfast.

A few steps later inside the bathroom, I put the comb to work then doused my face with cold water. It seemed to bring me back to life, but of course it didn't. I was still lying in that hospital bed. And as I watched myself dry my face in the mirror, that again was front and center in my mind. Sure, other than riding out that storm, I'd been having a terrific time. But there also were those times when I wondered who the hell I was and who I might have left behind. Blotting my temples now, I had a very unsettling revelation. It had to do with yet another question—where am I going to end up in a few days? Not knowing myself from Adam, I really didn't much care whether it was up in Ernest's neck of the woods or back in my previous life. If push came to shove I would have chosen to stay on earth so as not to hurt my mystery wife. But suddenly now, that other possibility popped into my head.

What if I wind up or possibly down . . . in hell! Shit, I never thought of that one. I don't even know who I am. I don't have a clue as to what I've done in the past. I mean . . . I seem like a decent person. I don't think I would ever do anything terribly bad.

Those thoughts, along with visions of demons and hell's flames, followed me when I left the bathroom. But as I coursed the length of the crowded bar for the second time and saw Ernest at the far end of it again, every bit of my hell-fueled anxiety vanished as quickly as it had appeared. His guest had arrived, and I just had to smile again.

Well I'll be! Look who it is!

Sitting on Ernest's right, with a wide smile and a tattered white captain's hat tilted back on his head, was none other than Sloppy Joe Russell. His arm was clenched around his longtime friend's shoulders, and they were laughing hysterically.

Chapter 8

"Josie," Ernest said as I came up to them, "I want you to meet Jack Phelan. Jack, this is Josie Russell."

Holding onto his smile, he rose from his stool and offered me his hand.

"Real good to meet you, Jack. I've heard a lot about you."

"It's nice to meet you, too, Mister Russell."

"You can deep-six the Mister stuff, Jack. Please . . . just call me Joe or Josie."

"Okay, Joe," I said as we both took our seats.

"What's my buddy here been telling you? I wasn't gone very long. He couldn't have torn me apart too badly."

"Heh, heh," the longtime rumrunner chuckled. "No, it wasn't Papa who filled me in. It was the main man upstairs."

Joe's mention of "the main man" reminded me of my predicament yet again. Feeling that frame of darkness bordering my good mood again, I said, "Well, I certainly hope it wasn't too bad."

"Nah, don't worry about it, Jack. Just keep sailing along for now. Be yourself."

"Yeah, whoever that is," I said.

Ernest and Joe got a rise out of that one. But their laughs were infectious. Loosening up a bit, I chuckled along with them as the bartender finally made his way over to us.

In a Casablanca-secretive voice, almost a whisper, the bartender said, "Meester Hemingway and Meester Russell, it is good to see both of you again. I know what you gentlemen prefer to drink, but what would you like, Jack?"

With my eyes gone buggy, I looked at the red-jacketed, Cuban mixologist.

The lean, dark-skinned, fiftyish man looked as if he might have been quite the ladies' man at one time. With just a touch of gray in his temples, the rest of his hair was lustrous black and combed back. He also had a neatly trimmed moustache and a smooth manner. I instantly thought, "Now here is a man of great confidence."

I told him, "I'll have a bottle of beer, whatever you recommend."

"Coming right up," he said, extending his hand over the bar. "I am Humberto Salazar, Jack. I am very pleased to meet you."

"Same here. My pleasure."

Then, winking at Ernest and Joe, he said, "I will be right back with your drinks, my friends."

"Holy mackerel!" I said after he left, "You guys have one heck of a network down here, don't you?"

"If you only knew," Sloppy Joe said, his smile now taking on an ironic edge.

"Forget all that for now," Ernest chimed in before turning back to Joe. "You have to get to know my old compadre here, and I've got to take a good look at him. It's been a long, long time, partner. How have you been?"

"You bet it's been a long time," Joe said, now losing the smile completely, "and I'm not very happy about it either."

"What are you talking about? Not happy about what?" Ernest came back.

"Hell, man, I kicked the bucket twenty years before you did. I died in '41, and you went in '61, right?"

"Yes?"

"Well, I didn't make the trip *up* until ten years *after* you. I just got there last September."

"Yeah, I heard you were around. I'm sorry Josie, but He had me so busy I haven't had time to run you down."

"Don't worry about that. I'm just saying; I had to do seventy years in purgatory. The average stint is just thirty to forty. Nothing personal, you know I love you and all that, but you only did forty."

"The suicide thing was one of the big reasons why I did time. What the hell did you do, Josie. Who'd you kill?"

"Get out of here, nobody."

Then Sloppy Joe Russell paused for a moment. With the look of a man who'd searched his past many times before, he seemed to again be inventorying his darkest memories. Then he said, "Nobody. I never killed anybody. Not that I know of, anyway. You know how it is. They never tell you *why* you're in the halfway house. Just as they don't tell you when you'll be getting out."

"I think that's the point, Josie." Ernest interjected, "We were put there to reflect, to ponder, and to repent. Obviously you did *something* right, or He wouldn't have let you out."

Sitting on my stool, taking all this in, I realized there was now a fourth direction that my fate could head in. Thankfully, I didn't have to dwell on it too long. Ernest quickly took the conversation in another direction.

"Come on, Josie," he said patting his back with a beefy hand, "let it go, man. You know how He is. Like they have always said—He works in strange ways."

"Ahhh hell, Hem, I suppose you're right. All that's behind me now, isn't it? It's behind both of us."

Finally allowing himself another smile and brightening our moods once again, he said, "Man, it's good to see you?"

Then Humberto returned with the drinks, but before serving them he carefully laid three coasters on the bar.

"Would you look at that?" Ernest said. "The coasters have my signature on them! Hey, Humberto, tell the boss he should be giving me a cut of the take."

The bartender then smiled and winked. And the way he so gracefully and ceremoniously lowered my drink on top of the thin, round cardboard somehow made me feel special. He did it in a way that made me feel like he was awarding me the Nobel Prize or uncovering the Hope Diamond before me. But as thirsty as I was, I would have taken the moist cold bottle of beer over either one of them.

When he gave Ernest a Papa Dobles and Josie his beer, he leaned close to them and whispered, "Please, gentlemen, hold onto them so they disappear. It would look very strange eef anyone saw the drinks suddenly disappear when you pick them up, then reappear when you put them back down."

"I know the drill, my friend," Ernest said, "You don't want the whole bar thinking they're seeing things. They'd think they were seeing things, and the place would empty out in a heartbeat."

Ernest, Joe, and I talked for over an hour. For the second day in a row, I clung onto Hem's every word. The few times our high-spirited banter subsided, we hit on a few more serious subjects. When we did, Ernest's remarks would become as terse as his famous writing style. His tone took on a serious edge, and he didn't waste a single syllable. Not only that but every comment he made seemed to carry an invaluable lesson. I felt privileged to be sitting alongside him, and there were times when I felt like the three of us were living out a scene in one of his novels.

Sloppy Joe was a good storyteller in his own right. He may not have expressed himself as eloquently as his best friend could, but it was obvious he, too, was a wise man. He had that far-reaching kind of wisdom that just cannot be learned in university classrooms. Much of what Joe Russell had learned in his lifetime he'd picked up by taking risks and spending countless hours in barrooms. Nevertheless, he'd always been a good family man. And when he spoke about his three children, his voice filled with pride.

But there were also times when his words and gestures burst with excitement. He really got worked up while telling some wild and wooly tales about his middle-of-the-night, rum-running escapades. When he mentioned a couple of Key West-to-Havana runs that Ernest had accompanied him on his boat, the Anita, old Hem got pretty keyed-up himself. Of course, he embellished their adventures and added small details that really brought them to life.

They talked about the Key West days as well. Ernest told me how he and Joe had become instant friends when, after a local bank wouldn't cash a thousand-dollar royalty check for him, Joe would. He also talked about the night in 1937 when they moved the bar's booze and furniture from its Greene Street location to Duval Street. He told how Joe had originally called his place The Blind Pig; then The Silver Slipper; and finally, upon Ernest's encouragement, Sloppy Joe's. They also talked about Ernest's "mob" of friends and about much of their tomfoolery. They had plenty of laughs when they spoke of John Dos Passos, Henry Strater, Waldo Peirce and all the rest.

But the funniest part of our get-together came when two pretty tourists from Quebec came over to us. Ernest had noticed them looking my way, whispering to one another, giggling and pointing in my direction. Minutes later, the slightly-intoxicated, strawberry blonde and redhead came over to me. When they asked if they could sit at the empty stools, I told them I didn't think it was a good idea. I said that one of them was reserved for Ernest Hemingway. They thought that was hysterical—until they tried to sit down. When they did, both of them received a little pinch. Not knowing what hit them, or I should say squeezed them, they shrieked together and lifted off the stools like two goosed frogs. When they landed, they headed straight for the door, and I heard the redhead say, "That's it. No more afternoon tequila!"

Though we had yet another good laugh, after it was over our conversation took a far more serious turn.

Humberto came over and said, "Excuse me gentlemen, but I've just received word that Meester Russell will be leaving in fifteen minutes."

Joe thanked him then turned back to us. He pulled the brim of his captain's hat way down low then leaned closer to us. Looking as serious as he must have while making backroom deals in the 1930's, he said, "Alright guys . . . time to get down to business. I've got to tell you the purpose of my visit."

Ernest straightened up on his backless stool. "Okay, Josie. Talk to us. What's going on now?"

"Well, He sent me down here for two reasons. One was so I could see you again, Ernest. But the other one, the main reason . . ." Joe said, now turning his eyes my way, ". . . was to find out what I thought of Jack here."

"No offense, buddy, but why would He care what you think of him?"

"It's like this, Ernest; The Man feels that Jack here is a pretty sharp troop. He told me that he's got a very sharp mind.

You might not realize that, Jack, because there's a lot you can't remember right now.   But He said you're a very insightful, articulate person."

"He said that about *me*?" I said.

"Yes. He also told me that even though you're a little rough around the edges, when you get into conversations with people, you're often two or three perceptions ahead of them."

Smearing a big smile across his face after hearing that, Ernest said, "See there, Jackie boy, you're not a total lost cause after all."

"Cute, Ernest, real, real cute," I said, nodding my head at him. Then I looked back at Sloppy Joe. "Did he say anything else?"

"He said he's taking a close look into your mind right now. Ernest might have told you, but he wants to be sure you have what it takes to write a very special book. And you were right, Papa. That storm you guys were in this afternoon—it was a test. He was reading Jack's thoughts and observations."

"I guess he liked what he saw," Ernest said.

"Seems that way. Jack's still here."

"I'm flattered, Joe," I said, "but why me? The world is full of good authors . . . experienced writers. What do I know about writing?"

He took a last swallow from his beer bottle, looked around to make sure nobody was watching then gently placed it on top of the bar. "That I don't know. Maybe it's the perception thing. Maybe it's because you're a big fan of my old friend here. Maybe He's considering you because you got into that accident.   Since you're in a coma right now you were available to come and meet Ernest. Maybe he figured Ernest would give you a few tips while you're together. I don't know His reasons. I can't tell you exactly why."

Joe glanced at a clock on the far wall then quickly turned his eyes back to Ernest.   For the first time since he'd come into El Floridita, they didn't look so cheery.

I've got to run, guys," he said, "but before I do, let me tell you one last thing. Ernest, this book He wants written . . . well, you've got something to do with it. It concerns you."

"Me? What in God's name are you talking about, Josie?"

"Sorry, Ernest, I've really got to run. Don't be mad at me. He told me that was absolutely all I could give you."

"I understand, Josie."

Joe Russell shook our hands. Then the two old friends shared a long, hard hug. When they released each other I saw Joe's eyes had moistened. And Ernest's voice cracked as he said, "I'll see you soon, Josie, real soon."

Then Joe vanished, right before our eyes.

Chapter 9

Minutes after Joe left the bar, Humberto Salazar came back over and offered us a ride to the Finca Vigia. Being it was five o'clock and the end of his shift, Humberto said he'd be honored to drive us to the hilltop estate Ernest had called home for twenty years. Glad not to have to take a cab, we filed out of the restaurant and hoofed it three blocks to where the car was parked. The narrow streets were lined by tenements and filled with playing children. Little girls jumped rope, and barefoot boys screamed and yelled as they cooled off in the rushing water of an open fire hydrant. As we made our way down a sidewalk, the smell of hot Cuban food wafted from open windows along with the lyrics of Creolized Caribbean music.

"Look, Senor Ernest," Humberto said, pointing to a two-toned orange and beige car parked up ahead. "It is a surprise."

"Get out of here!" Ernest came back. "It can't be!"

"Oh, but it is."

Wedged between two other cars alongside the curb was a 1955 Chrysler New Yorker Deluxe convertible.

"Well I'll be! My old car! I used to shuttle my son Gigi's entire baseball team in this."

With the top down, the upholstery looked every bit as new as the body Ernest was by now caressing.

"Son of a gun," he said. "It's been restored."

"Yes," Humberto said before taking one last drag from his filtered cigarette and flicking it into the gutter. "I would let you drive it home, but I fear we might be stopped by the police."

"Can you imagine that," Ernest said, "a driverless car in the streets of Havana. That would put the Headless Horseman to shame." Then he looked at me.

"Couldn't you just see the look on our taxi driver's face if he saw that one, Jack?"

We had a good chuckle while Humberto side-stepped between two close bumpers to get to the driver's side. "Come," he said, "we should get going. It ees a thirty-minute drive."

I opened the passenger door to get into the back seat, but Ernest stopped me.

"I'll sit back there," he said, resting a heavy hand on my shoulder. "That might look somewhat odd too . . . you in the back and Humberto up front."

Light as the Havana traffic was, before we knew it we were out of the city. It was still warm, but when we picked up speed in the countryside, the breeze rushing into the open car refreshed us all. Nobody said much, but I turned back toward Ernest twice and saw he was taking everything in. Seeing he was in a pensive mood, I left him alone to reminisce.

As we closed in on Ernest's old estate surrounded now by lush, tropical greenery, I looked for a tall hill. I knew that Finca Vigia was Spanish for Lookout Farm and that it sat atop a hill. But before I could see the house, Humberto slowed the Chrysler to a stop on the country road. He shifted the transmission into park then turned to look at Ernest in back.

"As you know, Senor Hemingway, the entrance is but another mile from here. Come . . . why don't you drive your car the rest of the way? It is very quiet here. I do not think anyone will see you."

"Sure. What the hell."

I got out and opened the door for Ernest, and he pulled his stiff body out of the car. Then Humberto climbed out, and Ernest slid behind the wheel. Our Cuban friend closed the door and said, "I will be leaving you gentlemen now." Then he shook our hands.

"It's a long walk back, Humberto," I said, winking at him as if I were now an insider.

"Oh, I will make it."

He gave the door a gentle pat then started walking back toward Havana. We turned and watched him for a moment. He was something else. All spruced up in his red jacket and fine black trousers, he strolled down that long country road as if he didn't have a care in the world. When Ernest pulled away, I looked back at him one more time. Humberto Salazar was nowhere to be seen. I let out a sigh, and Ernest glanced in the rearview mirror and only smiled.

A hundred yards later we rounded a curve, and Ernest said, "Now *this* is going to be interesting, Jacky boy."

Up ahead, on the driver's side of the road, an old man ambled along with four goats.

"Watch his eyes," Ernest said as he slowed the car down.

When we got close enough so that the old timer could hear us coming, which was just before we passed him, he stopped and turned our way.

Fighting back the laughter by now and with a goofy smile on my face, I gave him a little wave.

His eyes were disinterested. They followed us as we went by, but that was it. He acted as if he'd seen a hundred driverless cars on that quiet road every day.

When we passed him, Ernest and I both popped a gut. Like two wild and crazy teenagers in daddy's convertible, we roared and chortled as we bounced in our seats. Finally, after half-pulling ourselves together, Ernest said, "Talk about being world weary," and we lost it all over again. Life, or whatever state of existence I was in, was good.

About the time we regained our composure again, Ernest stomped the brake pedal.

"I don't believe I almost missed it," he said, turning the wheel hard right and pulling into a break in the trees. As we rolled to a stop, he said, "There we go. Jump out and open the gate."

It was a wide metal gate like you'd expect to see at a ranch's entrance. There was a shield mounted on the middle with the letters FV emblazoned on it. Behind that, a narrow sandy road cut through a pine forest. I couldn't yet see the house or any outbuildings. As we idled slowly ahead, I could tell Ernest's anxiety was building. There was tension in the air just as there had been when we'd walked up to the front door of his Key West home. Apprehension was smeared all over his face. He looked like he was pushing the car rather than driving it.

"Are you okay?" I asked.

He turned to me, giving me a slow wink that said, "Thank you, and yes, I'm alright." We then rounded a bend. He looked a little stronger, and he said, "There she is . . . to the left up there. All cleaned up, sitting proud beneath her protective shelter."

It was the Pilar. Seeing the boat there on a concrete pad surrounded by tall swaying bamboo did not surprise me in the least. Not much would at this point.

"The swimming pool is in the trees there as well," Hem said. "I buried some of my pets right near it. Hell, I even had gravestones made for them." After seemingly reflecting back in time for a moment he added, "See the tower over there? Mary had it built so I could write in it. But I couldn't work in there. Eventually the cats took it over."

"This sure is one beautiful place."

"Yes it is. At first I thought I wouldn't like it, you know, being so far from town. But we had many good times here. Hey, there it is. There's the house!"

Tinted pink by the setting tropical sun, the stone building was magnificent. Edged on the sides by palm trees, the place resembled a single-story fortress with a second floor on just one end. Stone steps almost as wide as the horizon led up to a huge front patio. Sitting atop the high wooded grounds like it had since 1886, the Finca Vigia looked every bit the paradisiacal writer's home it had once been.

Ernest said nothing. He parked the car, and we walked to and up the steps to the spacious courtyard. Still not muttering a word, he accessed his surroundings. When he finally finished, he let out one low grunt, and I then followed him to a smaller set of steps leading to a pillared entryway. Once we were inside the house, I again stayed in the living room while he roamed around. Not knowing what to expect, I minded my own business and looked around some.

Just like his Key West home, this one was very airy with tall ceilings and lots of windows. Beneath the windows on one wall, a long bookcase full of Ernest's favorite reads stretched almost the entire length of the room. I touched some old book covers; then I pulled two out. They were The Brothers Karamozov and James Joyce's short story collection Dubliners. Both looked like they had been individually cleaned. Several trophy animal heads adorned the uncluttered walls along with a few pictures. The period furniture was sparsely arranged, and a well-stocked bar took up most of one side wall.

Even though the old place lacked air-conditioning, it was cool in the spacious room as I walked around with the knowing grin of an inside trader. When the welcome smell of hot Cuban food drifted in from another room, that grin stretched into a smile. Nodding my head I muttered, "Mmm hmm, dinner's on."

Suddenly appearing in the room like a, well . . . like a ghost, Ernest said, "Everything looks to be in shipshape, Amigo. What do you say I mix us both one before we sit down to eat?"

"Why not?" I said, parking myself in an upholstered chair by the bar.

"What's your preference?"

"Doesn't matter, whatever you recommend."

In a flash Ernest handed me a stemmed glass. It was a Daiquiri, complete with lime juice and sugar. He sat in the chair next to me, and I asked him, "What's the most important thing you can tell me about writing? I've been meaning to ask you . . . just in case."

Stirring his drink while he spoke he said, "You have to write about what you know. That's *the* most important advice I can give you. If you don't know what or where you're writing about, they'll spot it in no time. You'll come across as a fake."

"Must you have been to a place or experienced an event before you can write about it?"

"It's always better if you have, but it's not absolutely necessary if you . . . ."

Right then Ernest was interrupted. There was a knock at the door, and the loud rapping sound echoed throughout the spacious room,

"Who in the hell could that be?" Ernest said.

Resting his drink on a table between us, he got up and lumbered toward the glass paned door. As he approached it he said, "I don't see anybody out there." But then he swung it open, and the moment he did, an entire crowd of what sounded like fifty excited voices shouted in unison, "HAPPY BELATED BIRTHDAY ERNEST!"

Chapter 10

As I rose from the chair, my eyes bulged, and my mouth slung open. I simply could not believe what I was witnessing. One by one, dozens of people from Ernest's long-gone past filed through that doorway.

The first to come were his wives. In the order he had married them—Hadley, Pauline, Martha, and Mary—all gave the birthday boy a hug and a kiss. His last wife, Mary Welsh-Hemingway, held him the longest. Once all four of them moved to the bar in a cluster, the next person stepped inside. It was Gary Cooper. Tall and rangy with boyish good looks, his smile brightened the room even more. Then in came Marlene Dietrich—the famous German-American actress of their time. I heard Ernest affectionately call her "my little Kraut" as they embraced. After her grand entrance, two matadors in bullfighting outfits followed. Behind them were Charles and Lorine Thompson—two of Ernest and Pauline's closest Key West friends.

All of Ernest's closest pals, known as his Key West "mob," came in together. They were a jovial bunch, and though they were bunched together inside the doorway, I think it was Sloppy Joe's voice that shouted, "Let the games begin!" I may be uncertain about that, but I'm positive that, with a wide grin and a raised fist, Hem said to Josie, "I really should cool you for not telling me about all this."

Max Perkins, Hem's editor at Scribner's, showed up as did F. Scott Fitzgerald and his wife, Zelda. Gertrude Stein, Ernest's mentor from his Paris years, walked in with Alice B. Toklas. Their arms were locked together and both sported uncharacteristically wide smiles on their faces. It was as if, after many years, Stein and Toklas had finally broken out of a locked closet. Later on Gertrude would ask me how I got the nasty "Ernestesque" gash on my forehead.

When Big Skinner, the bartender from Joe's bar came in, the doorway suddenly seemed to shrink. He was a towering, imposing figure even if he weren't the three hundred pounds he'd been during his prime. I stood there in awe, wondering how anybody, no matter how drunk, would not be intimidated by this man. I also wondered why Big Skinner ever bothered to keep a baseball bat hidden beneath his bar. Later, when I shook his enormous hand, I felt like a cub scout shaking with his new scout leader.

A band cranked up outside on the patio as other guests streamed into the crowded room. The musicians opened with *Happy Days are Here Again*, and I felt a nostalgic smile rise on my face. I thought how perfectly fitting the 1930's hit song was for such an occasion.

As I sipped my second Daiquiri, I felt as if I were back in time. It was like being at a mid-19th Century Gala or Academy Awards ceremony. And I swear, just as the latter crossed my mind, who walks in side-by-side but Clark Gable and Spencer Tracy. Gable looked as dashing as ever. He had on a white tuxedo and the same ear-to-ear, gleaming smile that had driven generations of women wild. As Spencer Tracy shook hands with Ernest, he was beaming as well. I imagined Mister Tracy must have smiled that very same way the first time he'd met his longtime sweetheart, Katherine Hepburn.

After wishing Ernest a happy birthday and mingling a bit, some of the happy faces retreated to the patio. I saw through the windows that vintage lawn furniture had been set up out there. Tables and chairs had been arranged in a semi-circle facing the band, and some folks were dancing to the tunes. I watched Marlene Dietrich do the swing with tall, bearded Waldo Peirce, Ernest's artist friend who'd painted several portraits of him. Pretty Zelda Fitzgerald was out there, too, swinging away with a man I didn't recognize. Other couples danced the jitterbug while white-shirted waiters made sure the guests had drinks of their choices and plenty of hors d'oeuvres. As I watched the goings-on outside the window, I noticed two men in my periphery. They were walking toward me. It was Ernest and a handsome man with hair parted in the middle. The grand party suddenly felt like a Great Gatsby, East Egg bash.

"Scotty, meet my new friend Jack Phelan . . . Jack, Scott Fitzgerald."

We shook, and his hand was smooth as a baby's. A heart attack had ended his life when he was but forty-four, and he, along with his wife, were two of the youngest looking guests at the party.

"It's an honor to meet you Mister Fitzgerald."

"The honor is mine, Jack. Please, call me Scott."

"Okay. Sure."

"Ernest here tells me that you just might become a fledgling author."

Feeling a small rush of pride from such a possibility, I said, "Yes, that's what it sounds like if I have what it takes."

"Well, if you do, don't be like our mutual friend here," he said giving Hem a devilish look. "Don't be going out and getting yourself a new woman every time you write a big book."

"Go ahead, Scott," Ernest said in a half-joking manner, "I'd love to find out exactly how *you* kept Zelda so happy all those years."

"Touché, Ernest," Fitzgerald came back, giving him a playful pat on the back. "Nice stab, lots of thrust. I award you a point for that one."

"In about two minutes, I'm going to award you with a right hook."

The close friends shared a good laugh; then Fitz said to me, "Alright, on with it then. Jack, if you do attempt to write something worthwhile, you must live inside your book the entire time you work on it. You must take it to sleep with you. It needs to be on your mind when you go to breakfast, lunch, dinner, and to the market. The best ideas will come when you least expect them. And they will be short-lived. Write them down immediately. They are always fleeting and usually irretrievable. They will abandon you as quickly as they appear. You do not want to squander those golden revelations."

All in all, our talk lasted about ten minutes, about as long as it took Scott to polish off the Gin Rickey he was working on. But before he went for a refill, I picked up a few more invaluable writing tips. I also learned something else. F. Scott Key Fitzgerald was named after a famous song writer. His second cousin thrice removed was Francis Scott Key, the lawyer and poet who wrote the lyrics to *The Star Spangled Banner*.

Though Scott had spoken in a stilted manner, I liked him. And it was easy to see that his thoughts were every bit as stilted as his words. I knew, had I the opportunity to spend more time with him, I could have learned an awfully lot from this man.

A short time later, Ernest deserted me when poet Wallace Stevens stepped into the house. Since I'd read somewhere they'd once had a nasty fistfight, I watched their reunion very closely. I feared it might put an end to the festivities, but it didn't. They shared a rousing hello, spoke calmly for a few minutes, and then went their own ways.

I didn't have the opportunity to meet Pauline or Martha because they disappeared somewhat early. However, I did get to meet Hadley and Mary, the first and the last of Ernest's wives. Both were very friendly and interesting ladies.

But, odd as it may sound, the person who fascinated me most was someone I'd never heard of nor read about. Henry "Prof" Tobias was one of Ernest's more obscure Key West pals. About Ernest's age but in much better shape, he was almost as tall as Big Skinner but wiry. When Ernest called me over to introduce us, I immediately thought that here is a man who's been around. Dressed in blue jeans, a white tee, and work boots, he looked like the type of guy who not only could handle himself through any kind of tough situation but had.

"Prof" Tobias in no way looked like a professor. He had a strong chin and a lean-but-sturdy neck. His short, parted hair had kept its brown color except for a bit of white infiltrating his sideburns and temples. There were no scars on his face, but it was still a face that told you its owner had no room for nonsense. His eyes, always the most revealing feature, were intelligent but at the same time wary. And there were good reasons for that. There were also good reasons for Prof's four aliases.

Because his mysterious mortal life was over, he didn't mind Ernest telling me about it. He even stopped him a few times and interjected a few details himself.

Right after the one-hundred-and-sixty mile per hour winds of The Labor Day Hurricane of 1935 had subsided, Ernest trekked up the Keys to survey the damage. He saw the worst of it when he arrived at Matecumbe Key, eighty miles north of Key West. Seventeen feet of water had washed over the small island, killing two-hundred-and-sixty-five men who'd been laying tracks for a new railroad. Those down-and-out veterans, who'd been working for The Public Works for Veterans Program, lost their lives when the ocean washed over the small island.

"It was a horrific scene," Ernest said. "There were bodies strewn all over the place. We located sixty-nine, and Prof, here, almost became number seventy. Many of the dead were entangled in the mangrove trees that lined the shoreline. The men were gray and limp as old dishtowels. Their bones were broken, and, by the time we arrived, flies were all over their bodies."

"Yes, and I was out cold," Prof said.

"We checked them all," Ernest went on, "but it was too late. I was just about to walk away from Prof when I noticed a bit of seawater expel from his mouth. His breathing was so shallow I didn't even notice. But when I saw that water, I realized he could be alive. We went to work on him, and he suddenly came to. Then, when I wanted to rush him down to the hospital, he refused to go."

"That's right," Prof said turning to his friend, "I told Ernest I'd only go to Key West if I had a chance of remaining anonymous there. And going to a hospital would blow that chance. I'd go to see a doctor but not at a hospital. Otherwise I was prepared to die right there in those mangroves."

Together they went on to tell me how Prof had joined the Public Works Program to get out of Chicago—eleven years after he'd killed two men in a New York alley. Prof fled to

Chi Town four months after the incident when the law in New York was closing in on him. Then ten years later he left Chicago for the same reason. In both cities he spent most of his spare time locked up in a small apartment, reading the classics.

"He's read as much or more than I have," Ernest said.

And that was quite obvious. Rough and tumble as the former fugitive's appearance was, and despite having just a fifth grade education, Prof spoke with the knowledge and eloquence of an Ivy League professor.

He went on to tell me that his first and only wife died of tuberculosis when they were both in their early 20's and that he'd never married again. She was an American Indian, a full-blooded Mohegan who'd grown up in Montauk Long Island. And that is why he wound up killing those men years later.

Boisterous and drunk, they'd been cracking Indian jokes in a seedy Hell's Kitchen bar. When one of them howled with laughter and listed to one side, he splashed a glass of nickel beer all over Prof who was quietly sitting by himself. He didn't get all pissed about the beer but calmly asked them to please stop the Indian jokes. He told them that someone once very dear to him had been an Indian and that such talk salted his wounds.

They became rambunctious and started giving him a hard time. Seeing the situation was quickly deteriorating, he simply up and left.

"Left a full glass of nickel beer right there on the bar," Prof said. "There was no talking to those mindless cretins."

The two men followed him out of the bar and dragged him into an alley. That was where their lives ended. With Prof's rage uncontrollable, he killed them with just a few punches each. He told Ernest and me it wasn't he who had killed them; it was the enraged adrenaline inside him.

It was getting late by now, and I'd been so enthralled in our conversation that I hadn't noticed that the party was all but over. Most everyone inside the Finca was gone. Joe and the *mob* were at the front door getting ready to pack it in, so Ernest went to say goodbye to them. I watched him take a few steps toward the men then turn back to Prof. He wasn't there. He'd simply vanished.

Scratching my head now, I turned back around toward Ernest. His mob had just filed out the door, and he was standing there alone. For some reason he suddenly didn't look all that good. No pun intended, but he looked as if he'd seen a ghost. Still near the bar, his body and eyes seemed to have frozen. As he stared through that open doorway, his face and eyes seemed a jumble of conflicting emotions. The most obvious was disbelief.

Then someone stepped over the threshold and into the house. It was a woman. And she had the same overwhelmed, wordless stare that Ernest had.

The woman, like everybody else at the party that night, looked to be the age she was when her mortal life had ended. She was ninety-two at the time. Tired as Ernest had looked in his final years, the lady he was now looking at looked considerably older.

Suddenly, as if meant to serenade them, the band outside came to life again. They started playing the very old song *I'll be Seeing You.*

The lady entrancing Ernest Hemingway was none other than Agnes von Kurowsky—the only woman to ever tear away a piece of his heart. They had not seen each other since 1918—since the day nineteen-year-old Ernest left a Milan hospital on crutches. Agnes, who'd been seven years older than he, was a nurse at that Red Cross facility at that time. And when she helped him convalesce from his war injuries, she'd gone far beyond the call of duty. The ironic part is that after she helped him heal, she injured him all over again. And she wounded him badly.

Once Ernest returned home, he believed the nurse he'd fallen in love with would soon join and marry him. But he was wrong. Shortly after coming back to the States, he received a letter from nurse Kurowsky. It was a Dear John letter. And it must have pierced Ernest twice: first when she jilted him and again when she mentioned she'd soon be marrying another man.

From what I'd read about their relationship, I'd always believed the scars that sheet of paper left on his soul were every bit as deep and painful as the scars all that exploding shrapnel left on his legs.

As I now watched, the two of them turned and walked out the door together. I wanted to go to the doorway to see what they were doing and to where they might be going. But I didn't—not right away anyhow. Still standing in the empty room, I just listened to the lyrics.

I'll be seeing you in every lovely summer's day;
In everything that's light and gay.
I'll always think of you that way.

I'll find you in the morning sun
And when the night is new,
I'll be looking at the moon,
But I'll be seeing you.

Finally the temptation became too much. I couldn't help myself. I just had to see what was going on. I made my way across the living room and looked out into the dark Cuban night. I could not believe my eyes. What I saw sent cold goose bumps up and down my arms.

Though the band still played, I could not see the musicians in the darkness. I couldn't see anything other than Ernest and Agnes. They were in each other's arms and dancing slowly in a cone of white light. It was as if a spotlight from heaven were shining down on them. It came from what appeared to be a pinhole high atop of the nighttime sky. Though it was very much like the light that beamed on the Pilar's bow that very afternoon, this time it was even more astonishing.

As I watched them dance, I had to blink my eyes several times. I also shook my head a few times—hard, as if trying to rid myself of a hallucination. But nothing changed.

Ernest and Agnes were young again. She was so beautiful in her nurse's cap and white gown. He was lean and dashing in his ambulance driver's uniform. And Agnes von Kurowsky supported him as he danced without his crutches. Cheek to cheek, as if they were one, they swayed gracefully in the light from above.

Then Ernest Hemingway leaned his head back slowly and looked into her eyes. He whispered something. She answered him. Then they both smiled.

Chapter 11

With my curiosity and amazement getting the best of me, I continued to stand there watching Ernest and Agnes dance. I knew I was intruding and had no right being there, but I couldn't help myself. Finally, after feeling my presence had desecrated something sacred for far too long, I forced myself away from the doorway and retreated to the sofa.

I thought I'd wait there for Ernest to come back in. Then I'd ask him about his miraculous reunion. How did it feel being young again? Do you still love Agnes von Kurowsky? Had you married her, do you think it would have lasted? Do the souls beyond the clouds ever marry? Do they love everybody the same? These were but a few of the things I wanted to ask him. But it had been a long, long day, and I quickly fell asleep on the sofa.

I slept through the night but have no idea how much of it I spent on that couch. For when I awoke the next morning, I was in a comfortable bed. But it was not in the Finca Vigia. It wasn't anywhere else in Cuba for that matter. It was more than a thousand miles away.

Lying on my back, the first vision to register through my squinty eyes was of yet another unfamiliar ceiling. This one had beams. Rolling to my side now, my other senses started kicking in. I recognized the incessant hum of an air-conditioner and felt a smooth satiny sheet beneath my bare thighs. Then I assessed the room. In the new day's dusky light I could see that the room was large and so were the furnishings.

I rolled over to my other side and saw another king-size bed there. It was empty, and there was not a single ruffle on the duvet that covered it. I'd wondered for three days whether or not Ernest ever slept. Now I knew the answer.

Over the steady whir of the air-conditioner, I heard a horn honk outside. Then another joined in, and they blared in unison. When the grating noise finally stopped, there were other honks but none of them as angry. I listened closely. There were busses and from the distance the shrill whine of a siren.

Beginning to wonder now where the hell Ernest had gone, I stepped out of bed and padded across a carpet thick enough to hide my feet. Pushing the drapes aside, I lifted one side of the window shade. It was lighter outside than I'd thought, but the sun was nowhere to be seen. Down below, a horde of tiny creatures swarmed the sidewalks. Between the wide cement walkways, I saw four lanes of frenetic yellow cars. As far as I could see, cabs were zipping, zapping, cutting each other off. My memory being what it was, I still didn't know where I was. But it all began to look vaguely familiar. By now the siren I'd heard had gotten louder. And just as a long, red, hook and ladder came into view, the door to the room opened. It was Ernest holding two white paper bags.

"Good morning, Jack. Hey, you're looking kind of good in your tighty whiteys."

"Cute Ernest. Real, real funny."

Lowering the bags onto a desk now digging inside one, he said, "Come on. I've got coffee and two of the best bagels in all of New York."

"That's where we are? New York?"

"You don't remember yet?"

"Remember what?"

"You grew up in New York, in Queens."

Peeking out the window one more time, I said, "I do feel like I've been here before."

"Well," Ernest said as he removed the top from a Styrofoam cup, "I've had a few words with the head man this morning. He's going to allow some of your past here to come back to you. It will come gradually, in bits and pieces, but as the day wears on, you'll remember things."

I walked across the room, fished my coffee out of one of the bags and said, "Where did you get this?"

"At New York's finest delicatessen. Wait till you taste the bagel. Hope you like onions," he said, unwrapping them both.

"Sounds good to me, but it must have looked awfully funny when two paper bags were flying along the sidewalk on their own."

"You know better than that, Jack. I just went for a little stroll. They were sitting outside the door when I got back."

"Don't tell me you guys have connections at that deli, too."

"We've got them everywhere. You'd be amazed if you knew how many people you've known in your life who are hooked up with us."

Sitting across the round mahogany table from Ernest now, I went to work on the bagel and asked him, "Well, now that we're in New York, what do you want to see first?"

Lowering his cup, looking at the dark liquid then looking back at me, he said, "Believe it or not, we're not here for me. We're here so that *you* can see a few things . . . bits of your past."

"I don't think I'll be able to remember anything," I said shaking my head.

"Oh, you will my friend; you will."

For a moment I wondered what I might learn about myself. But I quickly abandoned that thought and asked Ernest a question that had nothing to do with me. In a gentle, empathetic tone I asked, "What happened last night? With Agnes, I mean? Is it something you can tell me about?"

He took in a deep breath and held it for a moment. Letting it out really slowly he said, "Oh sure, I can tell you, Jack. But you pretty much saw for yourself."

Now, feeling as guilty as when I'd actually spied on them, I said, "I only watched for a minute or two, Ernest. Really! That was it. I felt like I was intruding."

"Oh hell, I don't mind that. To be honest, I didn't even think about it. I sensed you were watching, but my mind was deep into something else."

"What did you say to her? It's been what . . . almost a hundred years?"

"That's personal, Jack. That's something nobody other than Agnes and I need to know."

There was another brief silence. He ran a hand from the back of his head down over his white hair. Then he said, "Let's forget that for now. Did you have a good time at the party?"

"You bet I did. I met a lot of interesting people. That was nice of Him to throw it for you."

"It wasn't only for me. Just like this trip to New York, the reunion was for you as well."

"For me? Come on, Ernest. You know I never met any of those people before last night."

"Exactly! There you go. Like I just said, the party was for you, too."

Finally I realized what he was getting at.

About an hour later, after I'd showered and dressed in clean Dockers, brown shoes, and a powder blue button-down shirt, we locked the fancy room behind us.

We took an elevator down, and when we exited the Waldorf, a cab was waiting at the curb. Close to nine o'clock on a weekday, it seemed all of the people on the bustling Park Avenue sidewalk were running for their lives. Not one of the intent faces looked at any of the others as the charge of humanity sidestepped one another. Everybody was trying to beat the clock this overcast morning.

I opened the back door of the cab, and the driver looked over the seat at me. I ducked my head in. I didn't know what part of the world he was originally from, but his creamed-coffee face had the most disinterested look in all of New York.

Waiting by the door for Ernest to climb in, the guy barked through a bulletproof partition, "Are you getting in or not?" The impatient edge on his accented voice turned my mood as dark as his black hair.

"Relax, *my friend.* I'm getting in." And as Ernest scooted down the seat, I did as well.

"Where to?" he shot back.

He got me with that one. Not having any idea, I flashed a look at Ernest. He was fumbling with a small white slip of paper. As he looked at it he whispered to me, "Tell him to just head out to Flushing for now."

I did, and the Welcome Wagon candidate whipped away from the curb.

As we made our way toward the Queens-Midtown Tunnel, there was a grim look on the city that never sleeps. Lifeless gray clouds hung so low that the tops of the towering buildings were lost in them. All the pedestrians on the streets and sidewalks looked just as lost. Granted, most of them still walked quickly, but their steps had no bounce.

Just before reaching the tunnel, the lowest cloud opened up. There was no downpour, but the rain was substantial and steady. As it almost always does when rain falls on Manhattan, traffic immediately came to a near standstill. And just as it stopped, something else finally started to move—my memory. The first full recollection of my New York past appeared in my mind.

Wait a minute. I remember this. I remember traffic stopping in the rain. I remember passengers getting out of taxis before reaching their destinations and walking the last legs of their trips rather than sitting idle with the meters running. That's it . . . I was a cab driver at one time! Let me see. I think I did it for a couple of years. Yeah, I did when I was a younger guy in my early twenties. Hell yes, I remember that.

Entering the Midtown Tunnel by now, we were quickly picking up speed. The tunnel's tiled walls seemed to squeeze the two narrow lanes as we raced through with our headlights on. But it was a short ride beneath the East River's polluted waters. In a matter of just a few minutes, we were back in the dim daylight, motoring east on the Long Island Expressway. Ernest and I hadn't exchanged a word up to this point, and the driver hadn't given us a single glance in the rearview.

I'd been sitting on the edge of the back seat, peering out the window, and looking for more clues to who I was. They were coming more and more frequently; and by the time we neared Flushing, I was being bombarded with them. Scenes and incidents rushed at me from both sides of the busy highway. As cars, trucks and busses whizzed all around the cab, things were beginning to make sense.

Citi Field rose from a landscape of dusky tenements, and I remembered that Shea Stadium had once stood there. Then we swung onto the Van Wyck Expressway, and I saw the twelve-story-high Unisphere. The remnant from the 1964-65 World's Fair jogged my memory again. It brought me back to my childhood when my friends and I rode bicycles through the park that sits on the old fairgrounds. A small smile was growing on my face, but the driver quickly put an end to its future.

"Okay," he snarled without looking back. "Where in Flushing do you want to go? I must know what exit to get off here."

I pulled out the directions Ernest had given me when we'd left the Waldorf. Unfolding the strange parchment and feeling its smoothness with my thumbs and forefingers, I read the elegant handwriting again. "One-forty-one-dash-eleven Frankfort Avenue," I snapped as if shoving the address at the driver.

He continued driving without as much as a flinch. I turned to Ernest and gave him a sly little wink, but it didn't get the rise from him I'd expected. Instead he lifted his white brows and nodded his head pensively. Looking into my eyes as if reading the thoughts behind them, it was plain to see he hadn't appreciated my sharp comeback to the driver. I was surprised and disappointed by his reaction. But what had he expected me to do? Treat the guy like royalty? He sure as hell hadn't been nice to me. I just nodded at Ernest and turned toward my window again.

A few miles farther we got off the expressway at the Northern Boulevard exit; and as we entered into Flushing, I suddenly had to squint. A shiny, bright sun was finding its way out from behind the clouds. All the grayness was thinning, and splotches of blue were spreading. But at the same time, it started to rain—inside my head, that is. As we sped between Northern Boulevard's two endless rows of stores and old brick buildings, a deluge of nostalgic memories pelted my mind.

Oh wow! I remember that auto parts store! I fell off Eddie Carlin's motorcycle right in front of it. He was trying to teach me to drive that monster. Hey, look over there! That's where Horn and Hardart's restaurant used to be. We used to cut classes . . . go there for coffee and English muffins. And look at that . . . my school. Good old Flushing High. Hot damn, I remember it! It's the oldest public high school in all of New York. It still looks the same . . . just like a medieval castle. Yupper, it's all coming back now. . . .

The cabbie made a sharp right turn by the YMCA, and we were on a quieter, two lane now, surrounded by five- and-six-story brick tenements.

Look at that! Weeping Beech Park! There are the basketball courts behind the high cyclone fence. We used to have some damn good games there. I see the walkway still runs alongside the courts. Oh shit . . . I remember something about that that I wish I hadn't. After partying in Manhattan one night, me and the guys took a cab all the back way here. All of us were broke, so we got out of the cab, reached in our pockets as if we were going to pay, then ran like hell through the walkway. Poor guy couldn't drive the cab on it and chase us. Damn! That was a cold thing to do.

A few blocks farther the driver hung a left onto Frankfort Avenue. It seemed like just yesterday that I'd lived in the canyon of tall brick tenements before us. The building I grew up in was only three more blocks away.

We passed the schoolyard where all the bad-asses used to sniff glue and Carbona Cleaning Fluid. Across the street from it, the little Associated Food Store where I had my first part-time job was gone. I'd stocked shelves and lugged heavy egg crates there when I was fifteen. For the first time in many years, I could now see in my mind the pretty blond girl who used to come in three times a day to peek down the aisles at me. But I saw another thing, too. Something I didn't want to. It was me, planting cold beer and cigarettes in with the trash before taking it out some nights.

Then I noticed the dry cleaning store. And I recalled dropping bloodied shirts off there—more than once. It had been a mixed up time in my life when I was getting into far too many fights. Sure, I was young back then. But how would *He* feel about these things I was now remembering? How would they influence His decision when he was ready to decide my fate? How many other things had I done that crossed the forbidden border between mischief and trouble? Would more dark events come back to me—worse things?

As we made our way closer to my old place, I wanted to block all that out. I tried to bring back different memories . . . better ones of the twenty years *since* my departure from this neighborhood. But I couldn't bring back a single one. All I could do at this point was hope I'd turned myself around—behaved decently, and possibly made some retribution. Time would tell, but it was running out.

"It's right up here," I whispered to Ernest.

Again he looked at me as if he knew exactly what I'd been thinking, and much, much more. Maybe he did; maybe he didn't. But I didn't like the way he looked. I swallowed hard, pulled my eyes from him and turned them to the back of the driver's head.

"It's right up here," I said. "Fourth building on the right."

"I know," the taxi driver came back. "I know exactly where it is."

Sure, I thought. *How the hell do you know?*

Slowing down as we approached the building, he added, "I know because He told me."

I jerked my head toward Ernest. He shrugged his shoulders. Then he spoke for the first time.

"I told you. *You never know.*"

The cabbie then put the transmission in park, rested an arm atop the front seat and looked back at me.

"Of course there is no charge for the ride," he said.

"If you're in on this," I said to him, "how come you gave me a hard time when Ernest first climbed into your cab back at the Waldorf?"

"Because this was one of His tests. I cannot divulge any more than that, only that this was a test."

78

The cabbie was now speaking in a much more amiable tone than when he'd picked us up, and I realized that he was a pretty decent guy after all.

"Well," I said as I reached for the door handle, "thank you for the ride."

"You are welcome, but wait a moment. Don't get out just yet. I must ask you a question."

"Okay, sure. What is it?"

"Look closely at my face. Do I seem familiar to you? Do you think you have ever seen me before?"

"No. Not that I can recall. Why?"

"Because you have been in one of my taxicabs before," he said with an ironic smile.

"Really? When?"

"More than twenty years ago. I was the one who took you and your friends from Manhattan to that park we passed a while back. I was the driver you did not pay."

"Nooo shiii . . . . I mean . . . . You're kidding me."

"No, I am not. Do I look like I have much of a sense of humor?"

His white smile then spread cheek to cheek. It was a relief to see. Feeling somewhat off the hook now, I had a good hearty laugh. So did he and Ernest. I then got out of the cab, walked to the driver's open window and shook his hand.

"Thank you my friend," I said.

Still with that smile on his thin face, he said, "Have a nice day, Jack. Go now, see your old home." Then he drove off.

"Ernest, can you believe that?" I asked, joining him on the sidewalk.

"You bet I can!"

We just stood there looking around for a couple of minutes. Across the street there were lots of kids playing in the junior high school's big asphalt schoolyard. Outside it on the sidewalk, four mothers talked in front of the fence. Their small children suddenly began to scream as the bells of the day's first ice cream truck could be heard coming up the avenue. I looked beyond the kids and their mothers. On the other side of the high fence were the basketball courts where

I'd played a thousand games. The metal backboards, flush against the wall of an apartment building, took me back as well. I could again see old Missus Grabowski's angry face scowling out her fifth floor window. On mornings when we had dared to dribble and shoot before eight o'clock, she'd sit up there waiting for an opportune time. Then when we weren't paying attention, she'd empty a full pot of hot water down us.

When that thought dissipated, I rolled my eyes down the block a ways. The Christian Scientist church still stood there. And I remembered the countless summer nights when a mob of us teenagers would hang out on the wide steps—carrying on and listening to music from all the girls synchronized radios. When that vision ran its course, I turned away from the church and laid a hand on the mailbox alongside me.

I said to Ernest, "When I was a kid, I used to love to climb on top of this thing. I'd sit up here and be taller than any grownup that ever walked by. I felt like I was on top of the world."

Ernest silently nodded. Then he turned his head and eyes to the two big iron and glass doors to my old building. In a tone close to solemn, sensing the trauma of my homecoming, he asked, "Are you ready to go inside, Jack?"

Nodding slowly, I looked at those doors. "Sure," I said. "Let's do it. Let's go up to apartment 3-C."

Chapter 12

I pushed through the heavy door and held it open for Ernest. We then climbed the three wide steps to the building's inside entry doors that opened into the hallway. As I now held one of the doors open for Ernest, I did a quick study of it. The Carole Loves Jacky that a young teenage girl once carved into the wood was now gone.

Making our way down the hallway, we passed six, brown metal doors. All had the number one and a letter on them, 1-A through 1-F. We then entered the lobby, and I looked around for a moment. There were four more apartments on the far side and one small door that opened to a room the size of a phone booth. I looked inside. The old garbage chute was still built into the wall. I thought back to the countless nights when, after dinner, I'd fed brown paper bags full of our family's trash to the basement incinerator's waiting flames.

Stepping back into the lobby, I pointed to two iron radiators along the far wall and told Ernest, "When it was cold outside us kids would sometimes come in here and sit on those for a while."

Nodding his head, he said, "I can understand that. Nobody likes a cold ass." We shared a chuckle before he added, "I sure had my share of those back in Oak Park.

Ernest then stepped toward the elevator. "We might as well go up to your floor now if you're ready."

I didn't answer right away. I was eleven years old again. The unreliable elevator was stuck between two floors again. My pal Dino and I were going up to my place, and this time it stopped just before we got up there. We jimmied open the door, and there was the shaft's solid brick wall before us. Raising our eyes together, we both saw a two foot opening at the top. It was the third floor. Dino and I pulled ourselves up there and started crawling out. And at that very second that we pulled our ankles out onto the worn tile floor, the elevator started going down—quickly and with the door still open.

One second earlier and it would have severed us both at the ankles. Two or three seconds earlier and it would have cut our young bodies in half.

From that day forward, I always had an elevator phobia. I'd only get into one if it was absolutely necessary.

"Do you mind if we walk up, Ernest?"

Giving me a puzzled look he said, "Sure . . . we can do that."

As we approached 3-C, a small girl with yellow pigtails and excited blue eyes came out of the door next to it. Carrying what looked like a brand new doll, she scooted by us and scampered down the stairs. Obviously old Mister Brody no longer lived there.

Turning back to the door I'd lived behind for two decades, I gave it a good once over.

A silent moment passed before Ernest asked, "Are you going to knock on it, Jack?"

"I don't think so. I don't want to bother whoever lives here. Don't know if it would do any good if I did."

Again Ernest waited. We heard music inside. It sounded Oriental—an instrumental. It was light and soothing.

"You might learn a few more things about yourself," Ernest nudged now.

With the weight of what I'd already learned about myself leaning heavy on my mind, I said, "I'm not so sure I want to. Anyway, what're the odds whoever lives here is going to invite me in to snoop around."

He took a deep breath, exhaled and rubbed his temples. Looking down at a small black mat that did not say "welcome," Ernest came back, "Even the long shots come in occasionally. Go ahead. What have you got to lose?"

When he looked back at me I nodded. "Yeah, what the hell," I said and knocked three times, slowly.

We could hear footsteps coming now, very light ones.

Then the door opened slightly. A petite Chinese lady with ancient eyes cautiously peeked out beneath two brass safety chains.

"Yes? What is it you want?"

Feeling like a fool entering my plea through a four-inch opening, I said, "I'm very sorry to bother you, ma'am. But I . . . well, I used to live here a long time ago. I grew up in your apartment. I feel kind of foolish but was wondering if there's any way you'd allow me to see the place one last time. Like I said, it's been many years. I've left a lot of memories in there, and well . . . I'd love to bring them back."

She then looked me up and down for a few long seconds. I felt the guilty suspect in a police lineup. Finally she peered back into my eyes, drilling into them this time. Her small brown eyes narrowed more than they had when she'd first peeked out. Then she let me have it with both barrels.

"YOU CRAZY MAN!" she yelled. "GET OUT OF HERE! YOU NO COME IN HERE! GO! GO! OR I CALL POLICE RIGHT NOW!"

Man, did she turn out to be one heck of a door slammer. BLAM, right smack in my face! Tiny as she was, she heaved that thing so hard that the noise rang in my ears as it resonated in the hallway. On the other side of the door, three bolts quickly slid closed, and my scolding continued in rapid-fire Chinese.

"Thanks for all your encouragement," I snarled at Ernest.

He stared at me, and I stared back. Then we both lost it. We just cracked up. With the agitated old lady still carrying on inside, it was then our turn to scamper down the stairwell. Like two mischievous teenagers, we laughed hysterically all the way. By the time we made our way down the first floor hallway to the building's entrance doors, my abs ached as if I'd done two hundred sit-ups. We didn't even begin to calm down until we stepped back out onto the sidewalk. For a moment we just stood all hunched over out there with our hands at our sides and tears in our eyes as we tried to catch our breaths. And when we did, I knew I'd had enough. I told Ernest I was ready to go back to Manhattan.

We could have taken a bus to the taxi stand on Main Street, but I felt like getting a little exercise. My partner said he was game. He didn't mind walking and seeing a little more of my old neighborhood. With my sense of direction in working order now, I decided to take a short cut. We made our way through the maze of towering buildings, passed a Jewish temple, and finally came up to Roosevelt Avenue. When we turned there, I froze in my tracks.

As if the cement sidewalk had hardened around the soles of my shoes, my legs would not move. I could feel the warm sun beating on my face and on the top of my head, yet a cold chill prickled both my arms. Suddenly my mind came alive with yet another whirlwind of memories. Along with them, an entire stash of images flashed through my head. They were pictures of a person—just one person. She was someone I hadn't been able to bring back until now. Holding my arm out against Ernest's chest to keep him there, I stared at the second building up on our right.

"Good God, Ernest! That's where she lived when we first met! Right there on the second floor," I pointed, "the windows closest to us."

"Who? Who in the devil are you talking about?"

"*Blanche! Blanche* lived there! *My wife!*"

Chapter 13

As Ernest and I made our way past a drug store, a restaurant, a pizza joint and all the rest, I was far too deep in a funereal funk to notice the buildings. Sure, I was glad as hell that I'd remembered who my wife was and that she was such a kind, caring human being. She was a woman so good that her life had always meant more to me than my own. But it was also mentally paralyzing knowing I may never return to her. I'd answered a couple of Ernest's questions after we passed Blanche's place, but after that I could no longer make sense of his words. I didn't try to. I was too embedded in dark worry.

We'd been traipsing two full blocks down the gray sidewalk before Ernest's words began penetrating my consciousness again. He'd been leaning into my face and talking to me, but until now I'd heard none of it . . . .

"For God's sake, Jack, pull yourself together. Calm down, son. Nobody has yet said you're not going back to her."

"Nobody has said I *am* either," I came back, as we stopped to wait for a red light on the corner of Main and Roosevelt. Ernest said nothing more.

When the light turned green, we headed across the street and made our way through a flock of pedestrians crossing from the opposite corner. When we reached the other side, we passed a subway entrance and got into the first cab on line at the curbside taxi stand. The driver was a young guy with long chestnut hair and granny glasses perched on the bridge of his nose. He looked like a 1960's throwback. I figured he was a college student since there were textbooks strewn on the front seat next to him. The cab's radio had been playing loudly when we first approached, but he switched it off when we climbed in.

Ernest whispered from the side of his mouth, "Tell him we're heading to the Algonquin Hotel at 59 West 44th."

I did and then saw the kid's face light up in the rearview mirror. Manhattan was a good distance away. He'd be able to run up quite a few bucks on the meter. But he had other ideas.

"How about I don't turn the meter on," he said, now looking at me in the mirror? "I'll take you to the hotel for just a flat twenty bucks."

I turned to Ernest who was shaking his head no. He handed me five crisp, new twenties and whispered, "Tell him to turn the meter on."

I did. And on the other side of a glass partition the driver disgustedly flung the meter's metal flag up and "hrmmphhed" one time before pulling away from the curb.

"I thought you guys didn't deal with money," I said to Ernest. "You said you didn't carry any, didn't need to."

"When we have to, we do."

"Where'd you get it?"

Wiggling two fingers in the breast pocket of his beige safari shirt, he said, "I just reached in here, and voila, five double sawbucks." Then, in the same low voice, he said, "It's crowding two o'clock. What do you say we have a drink when we get to the hotel?"

"You bet! I can use a *few*."

Smiling now, he said, "When we get to the Algonquin, we can talk about what's bothering you."

"Forget it, Ernest. I don't care about the driver. I want to talk right now. He's not going to hear anything; he's got the radio going. He's in his own world now. And you know what . . . ? I really don't give a shit if he thinks I'm talking to myself back here."

I said that, but we still kept our tones low, and I glanced at the rearview each time I spoke. If the John Lennon lookalike happened to glance back while Ernest was speaking and saw I wasn't, well, good—let him think he was losing it. It would serve him right for copping a bad attitude.

In the back of the cab, Ernest gave me his fullest attention as I unloaded all my fears. Despite what I might have thought after reading so much about him in books, he was a damn good listener. Since I'd met him he'd never once tried to monopolize a conversation. But when it was Papa Hemingway's turn to talk, one listened closely. There was a good chance there was something to learn. And that's what I did when he gave me a lecture of sorts.

He told me that no matter how great one's fears are, it does absolutely no good to worry about them because if things turn out for the worst, nothing can change that. All the fretting in the world wouldn't help me. And, on the other hand, if things did work out well, I would be a damned fool to have made myself miserable for no reason. He also told me that he'd learned that lesson when he was but nineteen years old on the Italian front. When both his legs were full of hot shrapnel, he carried an injured soldier through a barrage of gunfire to safety. It was a lesson that had stuck with him for the rest of his life.

"Sure," he said, "throughout my lifetime many people saw me as insensitive. But that was only because I kept control of my emotions rather than let them take over me." He also told me the Silver Medal of Bravery he brought home to Illinois was nice to have, but the lesson he'd learned from the experience proved to be far more valuable than the award itself.

It was all good advice, and I was thankful for it. But I well knew it would take an awful lot of practice and willpower to make it work. Nevertheless, I made a mental note of all he'd said just in case I lived to write about him.

Our driver took a different route back to Manhattan than we took coming out to Queens. Because it was mid-afternoon and traffic wasn't all that bad, we were making pretty good time racing up Roosevelt Avenue in the shade of the elevated subway tracks. As I looked out the window, every city block seemed the same as the last, a blurred chain of parked cars and dark storefronts. But once we reached Jackson Heights, the monotony abruptly ended when I recognized one particular street intersecting the avenue. I remembered that for two years, when I had first met Blanche, I used to turn up this very same street five days a week to pick up my taxi.

Whizzing by it now, I was suddenly mugged by a memory I definitely didn't need. What I'd done back then was not an isolated incident. I did it three or four times a week. A driver from another shift had rigged the cab's ignition switch. It was set so that when the key was turned and held while driving, the off duty light on the roof would light up without turning the meter on. And I'd done it many times. It was the exact same thing the young man sitting in front of Ernest and me had tried to do on this ride. But back then I'd told myself there were plenty of other drivers who'd done it a lot more often than I had. I was like an alcoholic who always rationalizes when he sees another worse off than himself. I kept telling myself that at least I'd kept a handle on my larcenous habit.

Sitting quietly in the back of the cab with Ernest, I tried putting the advice he'd just given me to work. I tried to keep my imagination and fears from getting the best of me. It didn't work. And when we crossed the 59th Street Bridge, the lyrics of Simon and Garfunkel's classic song about the structure started playing inside my head. When they reached the part about "feeling groovy," I could only sneer at myself and shake my head in disgust.

Fortunately it was only a matter of minutes before we pulled in front of the Algonquin Hotel. The driver shut off the meter, turned to me, hiked his glasses up his nose a bit, and said, "Okay, that's $28.40."

I put two folded twenties into the small till at the bottom of his protective glass shield then tilted it his way.

"Keep the change, pal."

"Hey, thanks a lot. I appreciate that."

"Aaaahhh," I said, waving him off with a small ironic smile on my face, "just think of it as a *godsend.*"

And right then Ernest swung open the driver's side back door and stepped out onto 49th Street. I just sat still and watched the driver's reaction. His eyes popped out so far I thought they'd knock his glasses off his nose. Frantically he jerked his head and buggy eyes back and forth from me to the door and back again. Then the door slammed closed.

"What the hell?" the driver said in a near shriek.

"What?"

"Didn't you just see the door open and close?"

"Sure."

"What're you some kind of magician?"

Leaning toward him now and looking from side to side as if I were about to let him in on a big secret, I said, "No. I'm no magician. But I do know a thing or two. And one of them is that there are forces out there you *don't* want to be messing with. You *don't* want to be pissing them off."

"Whaddaya mean? What forces? Who are you talking about?"

"Just remember, thou shalt not steal. I'd start using that flag on your meter a little more if I were you." Widening my own eyes now, I gave him a big toothy grin and said, "See ya!"

I hauled myself out of the cab and joined Ernest on the sidewalk. The guy still hadn't pulled away. I turned to look at him one last time. He was nose to his window, and he was staring at me all goo-goo eyed as if I were one of the disciples. Ernest roared and patted me on the back as we stepped toward the hotel's front door. A doorman decked out in a dark, gold-trimmed uniform, hat and all like an airline pilot's, nodded and opened the door as I approached. Nodding back, I took my time so Ernest could whisk himself in first.

The Algonquin's lobby was nearly deserted. Subtly lit, the spacious room was elegant with all its dark wood pillars and trim. There were leather sofas, a few scattered palm trees, and a terrific old grandfather clock. All of it helped give the place a cozy, relaxed ambience. With Ernest alongside me, I marched up to a front desk that was as wide as some I'd seen in airports. A bespectacled, middle-aged lady waited there with a smile.

"Hi, I have a reservation."

"What is your name, sir?" she asked, laying her manicured fingers on a computer keyboard.

"Ernest, oh, excuse me; I mean Jack Phelan."

Looking over her horn-rimmed glasses now as if she were about to ask me if I was sure I knew who I was, she began to type. Feeling like a fugitive, a flimflam man, and a jerk all squeezed into one, the best I could do was offer her a weak smile. She accepted it and lowered he eyes to the screen. Ernest got a kick out of the whole deal and gave me a playful jab in the ribs. Without turning toward him, I snuck him a little elbow-shove on the chest.

Other than that, our stay was uneventful. We each had two drinks at the Algonquin's "Blue Bar" where some of Al Hirschfeld's art adorned the wooden walls. The bartender told me that Mister Hirschfeld had once been a regular patron at the bar. After he left to serve some other customers, Ernest told me that Mister Hirschfeld had once done a caricature of him for a magazine cover. He also said that Hirschfeld had passed away at the age of 99 a few years back and that he had seen him "upstairs" twice.

We didn't stay very long at the bar, and that was a good thing because when I got the bill for my two Corona's and Hem's two Daiquiris, I had to hand over every penny of our remaining sixty dollars to cover them and the tip. Reluctantly letting the bills slip from my fingers, I thought how nice it must be to live above the clouds where money is not needed. I also thought how, even though it sounded like my kind of place, I was still not in a hurry to get up there. The next day would be my fourth with Ernest, and I desperately hoped that when it ended I would return to Blanche. I wanted the opportunity to love her again. I wanted to be with her for many more years before being judged. I wanted; I wanted; I wanted, but that didn't matter. In our mortal lives we may be able to do some things that seemingly alter our destinies, but in the long run when it's all over, we take whatever comes at us.

Ernest and I hit the hay early that night. Check that. I should say *I* went to bed early. Because Ernest no longer required sleep, I didn't have a clue what he did. For all I knew he might have spent the entire night watching old reruns of Michael Landon's *Highway to Heaven.*

But when Ernest killed the lights, there were two things that I did know for sure. One was what he'd told me after we had dinner in the room. He said that *if* we did have one more day together, we would not be spending it in New York. The other thing that I knew, he didn't tell me. I observed it in our room. I'd had to repeat things to Ernest. I could tell his mind was somewhere else. He was jumpy as well. He kept getting up for fresh glasses of water he didn't drink, looking out the window, and constantly taking his eyes off the TV when he was in the bed alongside mine. He would stare at the curtains across the room, and I'd notice the lines in his weather-beaten forehead deepening. He was as nervous as I'd been in Flushing and during the cab ride back. The second thing that I knew was that wherever it was we were supposed to be going made Ernest very, very anxious.

When I finally lay on my side and tried to sleep, I wasn't exactly the picture of contentment either. An unruly crowd of uncertain thoughts kept merry-go-rounding in and out of my head.

Is Ernest's work with me going to be finished tonight? Will there be a tomorrow? Has he been ordered back to the hereafter but doesn't have the heart to tell me? Maybe that's it! He's not worried about where we're going; he's upset that we're not going. When is it going to happen? Any minute now? Am I going to make it back to the mortal world and be with Blanche again? God, I hope so. But what if that doesn't happen? Am I going to ascend to eternal happiness or spend all of eternity in hell's scorching flames? I can't even imagine how hot it must be down there. Doesn't your skin eventually melt off your bones? Oh shit, this is crazy. I can't keep . . . .

Eventually, I fell off.

Chapter 14

In the darkness, as if it were bashful, dawn's first faint, gray light revealed a small hint of the horizon. The dim glow seemed to be lifting the very edge of night's long, black skirt as it peeked from beneath it. I'd just opened my eyes and ears. The first sounds I heard were shallow water rushing over rocks and a choir of a thousand chirping crickets. After that I smelled something. It was the rich aroma of logs burning in a nearby fireplace. As I lay there on my side, the pale glow on the horizon afforded just enough light to reveal two huge silhouettes on either side of it. They were mountains, twins, and early morning as it was, they appeared to be black. It was cool outside, but I was cocooned in a sleeping bag. Beneath my hip there was a hard wooden floor, and I was peering beneath the bottom of a deck's railing. When I raised my head to have a better look around, I heard Ernest's voice.

"Morning, Jack."

I turned my head up and around, and there he was sitting upright on a long wooden bench. After trying to focus on him a little better in the darkness, I said, "Hey, Ernest, how are you doing?"

"I'm okay, all things considered."

"Where are we?" I asked, sitting up.

"Ketchum. Ketchum, Idaho. My last home. We're on the second floor deck. Did you sleep well? It seemed like you did."

"Idaho, huh? Hmmm, somehow I'm not surprised," I said, surveying the surroundings a little more. "Yeah, I had a little trouble falling off in New York last night. But after that, I slept alright."

I got up and sat on the bench beside him. Hunched over with my elbows on my knees, I turned to look at him. "Why are we out here? How come we didn't sleep inside?"

"I didn't want to go inside until it got light out."

Being it was so early and I'd just woken up, my mind wasn't yet running on all its cylinders. I missed his point completely. Not yet realizing the reason for his apprehension, I tried to be funny.

"You didn't want to go inside until it was light? What are you afraid of . . . ghosts or something?"

"Yes," he said, "As a matter of fact I am. But not the kind you're talking about. What I'm not looking forward to are the reminders inside and the memories of my last morning here."

"Oh, shit, Ernest. I'm sorry. I didn't realize. I'm not awake yet. Forgive me, man."

"Aaaaaahhh, forget about it, Jack," he waved me off. "I'll be okay."

Neither of us said anything for a while after that. The silence probably didn't last more than ten or twenty seconds but seemed longer. I felt like an A-1 shit.

Finally Ernest said, "This coffee was sitting here when we arrived, with this extra cup. How about some?"

"You bet," I said.

As he poured the steaming liquid into a cup, I looked at the tall metal flask he was tilting. I'd seen Ernest with it before in old black and white photographs inside books. I also remembered reading somewhere that for many years he'd taken it with him on many of his trips.

After we both took a sip of the coffee, he said, "Well, Jacky my boy, today is going to be it. I don't know when we'll part ways, but it can happen any time. It could be in five minutes. It could be tonight after you go to sleep. Either way I just want to tell you that I've really enjoyed being with you. We've had a few laughs, haven't we?"

"We sure have. And I want to tell you it's been an honor to meet you."

"Oh shit, Jack, don't start getting all sappy on me now."

"Alright," I said, raising my eyes from my coffee to the new pink light now splaying on the mountains, "but I just wanted you to know that. It has been an honor and a learning experience. Damned frightening at times and more fun than a barrel of monkeys at others."

"Well . . . if you do get to write that book He has in mind, do a good job. You've got the writer in you, Jack. I know that now."

"You do, do you?" I said, looking him square in those brown eyes of his. "How do you know? You haven't seen me write a single syllable."

"See that magenta light," he said, pointing to the top edge of the sun now shining on the horizon. "The Man responsible for that and all the other beauty on this planet has allowed me access to some of your thoughts."

Straightening up on the wooden bench now, I spun around.

"You mean you've been reading my mind all this time? Ever since we met in front of your House in Key West?"

"Come on now, pay attention to the details. Always observe the details. You know what they say about them." Lifting his white eyebrows now and speaking more slowly, he went on, "What I said was, He has allowed me access to *some* of your thoughts. And a few of the times when I got inside your head, I saw some very creative and insightful thoughts."

"I hope you don't mind me saying this, Ernest, but this gets freakier and freakier."

He said nothing. He just looked at me as if he knew exactly what I was going to say next.

"You're in there again, aren't you?"

"Go ahead, Mister Phelan," he said teasingly. "What did you want to say?"

"Oh, so it's *Mister Phelan* now?"

We both just looked at each other now. It was as if we were wrestling with our eyes to see who would give up first. But that didn't happen. Neither of us surrendered. Instead, at the exact same instant, we both let out a long, loud breath. "Pffffffffff," we sounded like air rushing out of two overinflated balloons. Then we let loose. We cracked up the way two close friends on the same humorous wavelength sometimes do. With his belly bouncing with each laugh, Ernest gave me a little whack in the back of the head.

94

"Hey! How do you know it doesn't still hurt back there," I snapped, and we laughed even harder.

When finally we calmed down, we were gasping for air and panting like two marathon dropouts. I wiped the tears from my eyes and managed to say, "Okay, okay, give me a for instance. Give me one example of what I've been thinking. Tell me something. C'mon, let's hear it."

With his belly still wobbling he said, "Alright, I'll give you just one. Let me calm down here; this is serious stuff. Okay, are you ready?"

"Yeah, I'm ready. Go ahead."

He raised his eyes to the small roof over the porch and kept them there a moment before shifting them back toward me. "Okay, I think I've got it right. Here goes."

At first I thought he was setting me up. I wasn't sure, but I thought he might go for an encore and try to make me laugh again. But he didn't. When Ernest spoke, the tone of his dead-serious voice put me to mind of the one time I heard him speak before we had met. A few years earlier, I'd heard an old scratchy recording of his Nobel Prize acceptance speech. As he spoke now, he used the same low, measured tone he did back then. His diction was actually reverent when he repeated the very first thought I'd had that morning. The illustrious literary giant looked out toward the new sun. With his craggy face and white beard tinted pink from the light, he put me to mind of Mount Rushmore in the early morning. But just as quickly as that vision had come, it disappeared when he spoke.

Slowly he said, "In the darkness, as if it were bashful, dawn's first faint gray light revealed a small hint of the horizon. The dim glow seemed to be lifting the very edge of night's long, black skirt as it peeked from beneath it."

Ernest then turned his head back toward me, and a small smile rose on his face as he quietly nodded his head. As if I were his protégé and as if he were damned proud of me, he then said, "Put thoughts like that on paper, Jack, and you'll have something. That is *excellent* stuff. A tad overdressed for me, but it's your style. And it's a very, very good one."

"You really do like it don't you?"

"Yes . . . . I do. And if you get to write His book, if you get that chance, always dig deep for your words like you did for those. Your sentences can't always be that flowery; only at certain times should they be. But don't worry, Jack, you've got good instincts. And they'll guide you."

Without realizing it, I turned my cup in my hands and watched the coffee slosh just as I'd seen Ernest do a few times.

"Thanks, Ernest," I said. "Thanks for your confidence." Then, looking at him again, I asked, "Do you think He's going to let me stay? Do you think He'll overlook the things I've done in my past life?"

"That I don't know. I don't know all the sins or infractions you've committed. We can never be sure about what He might do. But the way I see it, He must have known about your past before sending me down here."

"I sure hope you're right."

"I think I am. I also think He could have found out about your writing capabilities on His own. But He's got a big heart. Sure, He respects my opinion, and the feedback I give Him carries some weight, but I know, like I told you before, sending me here was a gift of sorts. Three days ago was the fiftieth anniversary of . . . of what I did to myself in the vestibule of this very house."

Ernest fell silent again. He was painfully ruminating over that most desperate of all solutions he chose that July morning so long ago. I said nothing. I looked out at the swirling, rushing river before us. Then I focused my eyes beyond it to the mountain peaks and said, "Are you ready to go inside?"

He cleared his throat then took his time getting his battered old body up from the bench. Then in an uncharacteristically uncertain tone he said, "I'm as ready as I'll ever be. Let's do it."

Chapter 15

The side of the deck we were on sat on a small hill. Ernest and I climbed over the railing then crab-walked down the steep slope. Reaching the bottom he said, "We've got to go in the back door. That's what Mary used as the main entrance after I died. She no longer would use the front entrance. She didn't want to walk through the foyer where I pulled both triggers that last morning."

Knowing there was nothing to say, I only nodded. With but a single long shadow following us on the damp grass, we made our way to a door alongside a pile of seasoned firewood. Ernest held onto the knob for a moment before turning it. He stroked the door with his eyes from the bottom to the top then held his gaze there. He took a deep breath and slowly released it. Then he said, "Okay, here we go."

Ernest acted as if he hadn't heard it, but the instant he turned that knob and gently pushed the door in, I heard the high-pitched cry of an eagle. It was directly over our heads and not very high up. Considering the intensity of this soul-stirring moment, I could only take a quick look at it. I couldn't tell the exact species of the bird, but it was an eagle. And the real kicker was that it was all white—a pure white eagle. Its body and wide, motionless wings were tinted pink in the sun's early light, but it was definitely white. Large like a bald eagle, it was even more majestic. My memory was far from perfect, but I swore there was no such thing as a white eagle. And as it glided in a circular pattern overhead, I noticed something else very peculiar. One of its large yellow eyes was trained right on us. As awestruck as I was, I still followed Ernest into the quiet house.

The inside walls were a blonde wood, and just like Ernest's other homes the furnishings were spare and uncluttered.

"I want to go upstairs first." he said without turning to me.

Patting the back of his shoulder, I said, "Go ahead. I'll wait down here."

He still didn't turn around, but he thanked me. And in that rolling gait of his, he lumbered across the thin carpet and up the stairs.

Slowly I ambled around the living room. There were large picture windows on three of the walls. They allowed plenty of light and views of the mountains that were to die for. All the windows and light walls may have made the room feel airier than it actually was, but the ambience was still somber and funereal. It felt as if I were standing in a well-lit mausoleum. Then it got worse.

I looked toward an open doorway and instantly knew where it led. Sensing that the front hallway was just beyond it—the vestibule where Ernest ended his own life—I was not ready to look in there. Slowly I turned away.

Alongside that doorway there was a 1950's style dining room set. Just beyond it, beneath one of the panoramic windows, a wide magazine rack had been built into the wall. Made of wood and looking like a rack from a public library, it was half filled with old copies of *Look* and *Life* magazines, yellow-bordered *National Geographics*, and various other publications.

Hearing Ernest's slow creaking footsteps above me, I stepped over to the room's only interior wall. It was solid stone. I ran my finger tips across one of the rocks and felt its hard, gray roughness. There was a fireplace at the bottom of the wall, and above it a portrait of an up-in-age Ernest. Next to the picture were two, mounted antelope heads. Like motionless sentinels, they seemed to be watching over the room with their dark glass eyes.

I was thinking how practical the backless bench sitting right in front of the fireplace was when I heard Ernest coming down the stairs.

He was holding up something small and looking at it closely as he descended the last few steps.

"Look at this," he said taking his eyes off it and looking over at me now.

"It's a pencil, Ernest," I came back in a tone that said, *so what?* "And it looks like somebody has sharpened it down to a nub."

"It's not *just a pencil, Jack,*" he said coming up to me. "It's the last pencil I ever used. I found it upstairs lying alongside my typewriter."

"Let's see. Hmmm . . . the point's pretty worn. One or two more sharpenings and you would have been down to the metal eraser holder."

With just an inch of the green painted wood remaining, I wondered how Ernest ever managed to write with it in his big, meaty fingers. But this trivial thought had a short life. It vanished as I suddenly realized the significance of what was in my hand. The simple instrument I was holding had been used to scrawl the very last words of one of the most influential writers of all time. As I carefully handed the green stub back to Ernest, I said, "That's right; I read somewhere that you based the success of your writing sessions on how many of these you went through."

"Yup," he said looking at it one more time. "I always considered a five-pencil morning a good one."

He then stepped over to the dining table, and with his lips slightly pulled into a satisfied, ironic smile, he said, "I'll leave it here for now. The house is in the hands of the Nature Conservancy now. If they want to put it back upstairs by the typewriter, they will. The main thing is that folks who come to visit can see this and realize its significance."

The contented look on Ernest Hemingway's face then began to fade. And it disappeared completely as he placed the pencil on the table. Suddenly he looked solemn. He knew it was time. Slowly, painstakingly, he turned toward the open doorway. As if in a gloomy trance, he stared into the hallway. A long moment passed. His eyes didn't blink, flinch, move or quiver. They just stared. Finally he said, "Here goes."

Then he took three slow steps and entered the hallway.

Immediately I walked over to a blue sofa by one of the windows and sat down. I neither wanted to see his reaction in that vestibule, nor did I have any right to.

It was quiet enough to hear a piece of straw fall on the carpet. I looked this way and that; I looked out the back window and then out the front one. I tried to focus on the mountains. I wanted to take my attention into them and away from this sad moment. I didn't want to hear my friend's sobs, but I did. I only heard three, and they were low, but they seemed to reverberate in the narrow hall.

When the sobs ceased, I felt relieved. Hopefully the worst was over. It was quiet again. A minute, two, five passed as I wondered what he was doing in there. I waited another few minutes—still nothing. I was concerned now, very concerned. Another eerie feeling wafted into the room then, and it hung in the stillness. I waited a bit longer.

"Ernest," I finally said. "Are you okay?"

Still nothing but silence.

Louder I said, "Ernest, are you alright in there?"

It was downright spooky now, and the concern in my voice had been replaced with alarm.

Still no answer. I'd had enough.

Pushing myself up and off the sofa, I rushed across the room as I shouted "ERNEST! ANSWER ME! ARE YOU STILL THERE?"

As I reached the doorway, the palms of my hands slammed into its frame to help stop my momentum. I looked inside. Ernest was not there. He was gone. He'd vanished. I didn't go into the hall. The thought entered my mind, but it didn't stay there. To step inside seemed like a blasphemous intrusion of a sacred place. And there was no need to.

The moment I dismissed that thought, something else hit me. I realized that Ernest wasn't coming back. But there was no time to mourn his loss or start worrying about what was in store for me. Everything around me suddenly started spinning. I gripped the doorframe harder, but it wasn't enough. My legs wanted to buckle. The room whirred around like the inside of an F5 tornado. There was a deafening noise. It sounded as if a hundred angry propellers were being pushed to the limit inside the room. The blue sofa, gray stone wall, dining set, pictures, brown animal heads, and all the rest whirled so fast they blended into a blur of colors. I couldn't hold on any longer. The spinning force was now too much. I lost my grip and was flung to the floor as if I'd been thrown from a possessed, runaway merry-go-round. Slam! I hit the floor hard. The concussion was so forceful that my head and body bounced off the carpet as if I'd fallen from a tall building. My arms and legs splayed as if there were no bones in them.

Then the lights went out. Everything went black.

Chapter 16

There was no light at the end of a tunnel, only that blackness. I couldn't feel any sensations in my body or mind, only nothingness. I have no idea how long I remained that way, but I don't think it was very long. Suddenly I heard something. At first it was very faint, as if it had come from a distant place. Slowly it came closer. I didn't try to determine what it was because I still couldn't think. I was just there and so was the sound. It was a series of faint beeps. Then they became a wee bit louder as if they'd moved closer. It was then that I felt something—two things really.

My eyelids flinched, and as I tried to help them open, I felt a pressure on my temples. Finally managing a slight squint, I could see through my eyelashes a dim light. Then I saw a hand in front of my eyes. It was a palm, and it was close. Its owner had his thumb and middle finger resting on my temples. The man said something I couldn't make out; then he slowly pulled his hand away. I could see better now. My ability to think was improving as well. My thoughts formed very slowly at first as if I were coming out of a long drunken stupor, but I was thinking.

I knew I was on my back in a hospital room. Then I realized the beeping sound was coming from a heart monitor. My eyelids parted some more, and I saw the man who'd lifted his hand. He had on a white coat. He was a doctor. And he was smiling at me.

In a soft voice he said, "Welcome back, Jack."

Sitting beside me on the bed, he was leaning in front of me. I couldn't see anything else. While his words, *Welcome back, Jack*, echoed in my consciousness, I suddenly realized something. He'd spoken with a Spanish accent.

As I studied the doctor's face, I felt my eyes moving. His eyes were dark and so was his skin. He had a lean handsome face, perfect white teeth, and black hair combed straight back.

I looked at the nameplate on his chest. In the green glow of the monitor, I could just make it out. It said, "Dr. Humberto Salazar."

Had I the strength I would have jumped right out of that bed. I could not believe who I was looking at. The more my eyes bulged, the more Humberto's smile widened.

"Get plenty of rest, my friend," he said. "I will check back with you later."

Then he looked at me approvingly, winked, and strode out of the room.

I now saw somebody else approaching. She too sat alongside me on the mattress. It was Blanche. She looked so tired yet still so beautiful.

"Ohhh God, Jacky . . . I love you; I love you; I love you!" she said.

Her eyes were as warm as they'd always been. No, they even warmer. Moist with tears of relief now, they sparkled like glittering emeralds. With her long auburn hair curtaining my face, she slowly lowered her cheek to mine. When our faces touched, I felt her tears on my skin and smelled the familiar scent of orange blossom on her neck. With her breasts soft against my chest, she rocked me, and I felt the weight of all the worry she had been carrying.

Leaning back, she looked at me again. Gently she stroked my hair. "I was so, so worried, honey. I wouldn't have wanted to go on without you. I couldn't have. We have far too many memories to make yet."

"You can't imagine how glad *I* am to be back, Blanche."

"I can't?" she said, as she softly caressed a bandage on the left side of my forehead.

"I'm sorry . . . . Of course you can."

We then looked into each other's eyes and shared heartfelt smiles. I wanted this intimate moment—this indescribable feeling of relief—to last forever, but it didn't. We were interrupted by yet another voice.

"Blanche, I have to run along now. I've got to check on some other patients."

"Oh!" Blanche said turning her head toward the lady who'd just gotten up from a chair. "Jacky, I want you to meet Desiree. She's a nurse here. I'd never have made it through the past four days without her."

Desiree, I thought, where do I know that name from?

"Hi, Jack," she said stepping close enough to the bed that I could see her. "I'm so glad you're doing better."

As I took her extended hand, I saw that she was tall and blonde. She had a harried yet kind look on her face, and her nametag said Desiree McCandless, RN. Somehow I sensed that I'd seen her before. I didn't have a clue as to where, but I knew we had met somewhere. Trying to bring her back was like struggling to recall a face from an old, obscure dream. I couldn't do it for the life of me. But then she helped me.

Just as Blanche looked back down at me, Nurse McCandless gave me a quick wink like the doctor had.

She said, "See you guys later," then turned and walked out of the room and closed the door behind her.

"Blanche," I said jerking my head up from the pillow, "I know her!"

"You know her?" she said as a concerned look spread over her face. "What are you talking about, Jack? You know her? You don't know her, honey"

Propping myself up on my elbows now, I said, "Yeah, I *do* know her. She's the waitress who served me and Ernest drinks at Sloppy Joe's."

"Sloppy Joe's? Ernest? Jack, honey, what in the heck are you talking about?"

"Sloppy Joe's . . . in Key West. You know where it is. We've been there together. I was just down there again a few days ago. I was with . . . with . . . well . . . with Ernest Hemingway."

"Ernest Hemingway! Oh God, Jack, you need some rest. Don't talk like that, please. You're scaring me."

Sitting straight up now, bouncing her upturned palms as she spoke, and fighting to keep her composure, she said, "Look . . . you've suffered a concussion. You've been unconscious for a long time. You must have dreamt all that."

104

The newfound relief was gone from her face now. The look that replaced it, I was certain, was the same fearful one she'd worn the whole time I was out cold.

"You've got to believe me, Blanche. I met the doctor, too. Ernest and I also went to Cuba, and Doctor Salazar was our bartender down there."

"Oh Mother of God, Jack, you'd better get some rest. Please, hon . . . get some rest now. I'll be back in a little while. I've got to go down to the cafeteria. I haven't eaten anything since early this morning."

She leaned down and kissed me. Then she raised her head back up and said, "I'll be back soon. You get some sleep now."

I did get some sleep, but she didn't go anywhere near the cafeteria.

Chapter 17

After two more days in the hospital, I was allowed to go home. I wasn't happy that Blanche had gone to talk to Doctor Salazar even though I knew he must have done his best to smooth things out. But there was something else that bothered me even more. The fact that my own wife wouldn't believe I'd spent four days with Ernest really burned my ass. I realized what I'd told her wasn't easy to swallow. But we'd been together twenty-five years—married for all but two of them—and never once had we doubted each other. That may sound like something out of a storybook marriage, but it's true. I've never known two people who'd been closer than Blanche and I. But for the first three weeks I was home, our bond, our unshakable trust, showed signs of deteriorating. After that things got even worse.

The events of my days with Ernest Hemingway came back to me slowly. No matter how hard I tried, I couldn't bring them all back at once. I'd remember an incident or two that occurred in Key West, as well as the other three places, but it wouldn't all come back in one tidy package. It was nerve-racking.

Every day, as things came back to me, I told Blanche about them. But she wouldn't buy any of it. On top of that, Doctor Salazar told me I shouldn't go back to work at my landscaping business for at least a month. And that didn't help matters. With the house seething with tension, we would have been better off being apart for a good part of each day. Blanche did return to her secretarial job at Luberdoff and Ackerly Accounting, but six weeks before my accident, they were forced to cut her hours. Thankfully the company was good enough to continue paying for our medical insurance, but now Blanche was only working four hours each morning. We were together all the rest of the time. Under normal conditions that would have been fine, but there was that tension. And it was pulling tighter and tighter.

Money was getting tighter as well. We were working-class people and didn't have all that much money put aside. That, too, did nothing to ease our anxiety. Neither did the first time I heard Blanche whispering into the telephone. I'd been in the spare bedroom trying to work on the computer, and she didn't hear me making my way up the carpeted hallway.

In a low tone that sounded both desperate and conspiratorial, she said, "This isn't easy to take."

Freezing in my tracks, I listened. She was sitting in the living room just beyond the archway.

"I'm sorry. What did you say?"

Then a moment of silence passed before she spoke again.

"He's still delusional. He won't let go of this damned Hemingway fantasy. I don't know how much longer I can take it. It's like I'm living with a stranger."

She then listened to whoever was on the other end. I just stood there listening to nothing. It took all the willpower I could muster not to storm in there, grab the phone, and ask who the hell was on the other end. But I didn't.

"Thanks for listening to me," Blanche finally said. "I needed to talk to someone."

Then she hung up.

"Who in the hell was that!" I demanded, stomping into the living room.

"Nobody. Just . . . just Susanne, Susanne Santos, from work. What were you doing anyway? Hiding in there? Spying on me? You scared me half to death barging in here like that. Don't ever do that again."

"You're going to tell me what to do?" I said, widening my eyes and standing over her now. "*You're* talking to God knows who, and *I'm* the one sneaking around? I don't think so. Now who the hell was that?"

Rising to her feet now she shot back, "I told you. Now get out of the way. And don't you stand over me like that *ever again!*"

Storming toward the kitchen then, she bumped my shoulder with hers. She picked up her purse from the table, came back out, and dug her eyes deep into mine as she rushed for the door.

Blanche came back a short while later. Needing to get out of there, she just went for a ride. But we didn't talk for the rest of the evening and half of the next day.

After I returned to work, things didn't get much better. And during the next two months, there were many more trying scenarios. Sometimes, even when things seemed to be going a little better, the smallest spark would set one of us off. Either Blanche or I would explode. The other would retaliate. Then one of us would either take off or go to a separate room. Either way, we'd both stew for what seemed like an eternity.

None of it was healthy for our marriage. And to make matters worse, I still hadn't written a single word. Not only that, but I was beginning to doubt myself as well. I didn't doubt as much as Blanche did, but I was allowing myself to think that just maybe the whole Ernest thing had been a dream after all. Maybe she was right. Maybe I never did meet Desiree and Doctor Salazar. Maybe, when I'd gone comatose, my mind simply led me to believe that I'd lived the entire experience. I was no doctor. I was no shrink. What did I know about how valid someone's memories are after they snap out of a coma?

Constantly I thought about this. As I labored in the torturous Florida sun—whether I was cutting people's grass, trimming bushes, or installing Xeriscapes—my mind ceaselessly turned the same heavy weight over and over. It was the same deal in my free time. All I thought about was whether or not I'd really been with Ernest. Like a closely balanced scale, my mind kept tilting this way and that. It happened; it didn't. It happened; it didn't. Then one Saturday afternoon it all started coming back to me.

Being an early riser I liked to take short naps on weekend afternoons. I would lie down for an hour, and if I fell off that was okay. If I didn't, that was alright too. Either way I'd get up feeling refreshed. On this particular day, I had just cleared my mind and was about to doze off when suddenly, out of nowhere, forgotten scenes from my days with Ernest began to appear. Rather than me bringing them back, it were as if they'd been delivered to me by some strange force. And all that passed in front of my mind's eye was highly cinematic. Clear as the moment it happened, I saw myself with Ernest at the wall of his Key West home. I saw all of what went on in Cuba, New York, and Idaho as well. Everything up to our departure in Ketchum was there again.

I sprung up out of that bed, slipped my denim shorts back on and high-tailed it into the kitchen.

"Blanche!" I blurted as she was finishing a hummus sandwich. "I've got it! Everything has come back! I can remember it *all* now!"

"Oh come on, Jack," she said, wearily lowering the sandwich to her plate, "let's not go there again. Not today."

"No, please, listen to me," I said sliding the chair next to her out and plopping into it. "I know now that it all happened. I'm positive. It's all come back."

Dropping her elbow heavily onto the table she wearily massaged her temples.

"Just listen to this, honey. Let me tell you just one thing that happened. Please!"

Without looking at me and her eyes still on the Formica table, she said as if exhausted, "Alright, just one incident, Jack. One last damned incident. Then I don't want to ever hear about it again. *Please!*"

I told her about the Pilar. About the tempestuous storm Ernest and I had gone through in the Bermuda Triangle. I brought back every sight, sound, smell, and feeling. As I told my story it were as if we were actually there. I painted that ink blue sky and the massive waves that crashed down on Ernest and me. I felt the electrical charge of the lightning cracking all around, the seawater over my ankles, and the unadulterated fear that had enveloped me.

And so could Blanche.

"Oh my god," she slowly said when I was done. "Jack . . . this is *scary*. I think I'm actually beginning to believe you. Honey, you could never have made up such a story. And . . .

and the way you tell it, it's as if you were reading the scene out of a novel. A classic. I didn't know you could do that."

"I didn't either. That's part of it, too," I said excitedly while bouncing my palms in the air. "I was there with Ernest because *He* thought I had a gift. *He* thought I had the talent to write a book about Ernest. *He* thought I should get to know him personally so I could show the side of Hemingway that few people realize existed."

"What was he like . . . Ernest Hemingway, I mean?"

"He actually had a soft side, Blanche, a very soft side.

Everybody today seems to only think of him as this burly, swaggering, hard-shelled bully. But that's all it was, a shell—a thin layer that was always tough enough to conceal the biggest part of him—the good part. He was a great guy, hon. There was more tenderness and benevolence inside that man than you'd ever imagine."

Weighing all this in her mind now—dissecting it, examining it, letting it sink in—Blanche said nothing for a moment. As she looked at me in the silence, I watched the face I'd known and loved for so long begin to return. Right there at the table and right before my eyes, the hard, scared, angry look she'd been wearing for two solid months disappeared. It was replaced with compassion. Knowing she was now with me on this, I was the one to break the silence.

"Thank you, Blanche. Thanks for believing me."

"Why did he do it?" she asked referring to Ernest's hard exterior again.

With all her doubts clearing away like parting clouds after a turbulent storm, her interest was piqued. She couldn't get enough. She wanted to know all about Ernest and everything that had happened. I told her all of it. And after answering her very last question, I told her what Ernest had said about the difficulties of being a man—how all through a man's life he instinctively keeps his guard up and how once his life is over and he faces immortality none of that matters and how only in the hereafter can a man finally be his true self.

We talked until late in the afternoon; and after I'd told her every last detail, she took my hand and led me into our bedroom. For the first time since I'd fallen off the lawnmower, we made love. With our passions fueled by immense joy and relief, we made Adam and Eve's first encounter seem like dull, casual, humdrum sex. It was fantastic, better than ever. And when we finished, our bodies still entwined, we lay there for a while.

Five minutes must have passed before Blanche whispered in my ear, "I want you to write that book, Jack. I want you to start first thing tomorrow."

Chapter 18

Although I knew nothing about the writing process and although for two full months I hadn't come up with a single sentence, when I sat down that Sunday morning, my fingers couldn't tap the keys fast enough. With Blanche now behind me and with my entire four-day experience sorted in my mind, I was flooded with ideas. All I had to do was arrange them in their proper sequence and bang away. Not being a good typist, I had to go back and correct mistakes in almost every sentence, but that didn't matter. Those ideas, words, sentences and paragraphs just kept coming and coming. And they were good. Damn good. When I reread certain parts, I couldn't believe my eyes. Some of it seemed so good it actually scared me. There were passages that to me sounded like they'd come from the pages of a literary masterpiece. And I wasn't the only one who felt that way. There were times when Blanche was absolutely stunned by some of the passages I read back to her.

She said more than just that once, "Oh my God, Jack. That sounds like you read it right out of a book!"

Crinkling my forehead as if I were already some kind of big time author, I'd tell her, "I hope so. That's what I'm trying to do . . . write a book." But inside I was aglow with a feeling of self-worth that I'd never felt before. I was so proud of myself. I thought that Jack Phelan—underachiever, Joe average, community college dropout—just might have found his niche.

As I am doing right here, I wrote about my four days with Ernest. But I did it differently. I went deeper into my beliefs of why Ernest had done the things he had. I gave *my* take on how certain events in his lifetime molded him into who he was. I told what I thought had made him tick, react, and become the legend and myth he is today. Sure, many before me had done the very same thing, but I had information none of them had. I *knew* the real Ernest Hemingway. And I decided that would be the title of my book—*The Real Ernest Hemingway.*

During the five months it took to do the first draft, Blanche continued to cheer me on. She was into the book every bit as much as I was. And she believed everything I wrote was true. I worked all weekend every weekend and a couple of hours after work each night. I even slept with a pad and pen on my nightstand. When those fleeting, golden ideas came to me, I scribbled them down so they wouldn't be lost, just like F. Scott Fitzgerald had told me to. I say the ideas "came to me," but each time one suddenly popped into my mind, I couldn't help but think they'd really been *given* to me. I don't know. Maybe my mysterious inner mind did think them up. But to be honest, every time I'd later type those thoughts from the pad onto the computer, I couldn't help but feel I was only a middleman relaying a higher power's messages.

Yes, the book was coming along, but not everything else was going so well. Our financial situation was quickly worsening from bad to dire. Blanche was still only working mornings. I'd missed that month's work after the accident and then only eased my way back after that. Our bills were stacking up.

Although Blanche and I had never made a whole lot of money, we'd always managed to stay on top of our debt. Somehow we always maintained an excellent credit rating. But things were changing fast. And for the first time ever, we were being forced to subsidize our income with credit cards. We had to make the minimum payments each month rather than paying them in full as we always had. Those balances were growing quickly. And about the time I finished the first draft of *The Real Ernest Hemingway,* things became worse yet.

They say that setbacks usually occur in threes. And in the past, Blanche and I had always believed that. It always seemed that when one unexpected expense came up, there would always be two more right behind it. But this time was far more financially damaging. We were hit by a long succession of unexpected expenses. Two-hundred-and-fifty dollars went to have one of my molars pulled. I could have saved the tooth, but it would have cost another fifteen hundred for a root canal and a cap. It galled me that a dentist could charge that kind of money for an hour's work and that hard as I worked, I could no longer afford to keep my teeth.

Then the transmission on my aging Ford pickup had problems—there went two grand onto the plastic. After that a wheel bearing in Blanche's Hyundai went, and I found out that my local mechanic had raised his labor charge to seventy-five bucks an hour. The expenses just kept coming and coming and piling and piling. Modestly as we lived, we couldn't even afford to subsist anymore.

But as I said, despite the relentless spirit-draining gnaw of debt, I continued to write. And it seemed pretty good. Out on the porch each evening before sitting down to dinner, I'd read my previous day's output to Blanche. And as the book's word count grew, so did our hopes. My first priority was to tell the world about the Ernest I had gotten to know, but Blanche and I also hoped we might make a little money from the book. All we wanted was enough to catch up on those bills and maybe, just maybe, get by with a little breathing room for a change. Everything was riding on the book's success.

I'll forever remember the day I finished the first draft. It was November 3rd. Figuring that it would take about another month to make the necessary corrections and add some polish to the manuscript, I first sat down to work on a query letter. I had to put together a one-page summary of my eighty-thousand-word story. And it had to be good. It had to convince literary agents that I had something worthwhile—something they would be confident they could sell to a publisher. Putting that one-page letter together turned out to be more difficult than writing the book itself.

It was nerve racking. How, in just a few paragraphs, could I possibly tell exactly how good the entire book was? I must have spent fifty hours laboring in front of my keyboard over that letter. Sitting in my garage-sale computer chair night after night and for two full weekends, I drove myself crazy reworking the query. The deletions, additions, sentence restructuring, and all the rest were maddening. Finally I finished it. I didn't think it was all that great, but I knew it was time to abandon it. I picked out fifteen reputable agents and prepared to mail the letter. But then there was another problem—another big problem. I didn't know if I should categorize *The Real Papa Hemingway* as a fiction or nonfiction book.

"I just don't know," I told Blanche as I popped open a cold can of Busch Lite on the porch one afternoon. "If I present it as nonfiction, who on earth is going to believe it? Who in his or her right mind is going to believe that I was in a coma and at the same time running around with a fifty-year-dead literary icon? If I say it's fiction, I'm not really doing the job I was given a second chance to do. He, upstairs, allowed me to come back so I could try to change the world's perception of Ernest."

"Hmmm, good point. I never thought about that."

"Neither did I until I went to work on the query letter."

"It's almost like you *have* to call it nonfiction."

"Yeah, I know. But you know how I was before I got the concussion. I was the last person on the planet who'd ever have believed in spirits, ghosts, apparitions and all that kind of stuff. I'd always discounted it all as mindless, hokey, whacko thinking."

Pausing then, I looked over the tops of the swaying Areca palm fronds between our place and the Weitz's next door. A cool front had finally arrived. After so many months of baking beneath the hot, unyielding South Florida sun, the dry comfortable breeze now coming from the north was a real treat. With the humidity gone, the autumn sky was now a deeper blue. And as I looked at it and tried to see into it, I said, "Heck, Blanche, before I got hurt, I didn't even believe there *was* a God. I wanted to but just couldn't buy into it. There was no proof."

I took a sip of my brew, put the can back down then looked at Blanche.

115

"Think about it now. If I ever do get the book published as nonfiction, what are people going to think of me? They'll think I'm some kind of nut-job. They'll think that . . . ."

"Whoooah!" Blanche interrupted. "Since when do you care what other people think? I thought we'd both gotten past that years ago. You're the one who's always said that you'd love to drop out. You're the one who's always said you'd like to have a few acres in the woods somewhere up north. And that you'd love to live with the critters surrounded by trees rather than people."

"Okay, hold on a minute here," I said, straightening up in my flimsy plastic chair. "You said *you'd* like to do the same thing if we could."

"Never mind. Forget that now. The point I'm trying to make, if you'd let me, is bigger than that. You now know there is a hereafter. You know there is a God. Why in His name would you, for the first time, give a damn what anybody thinks? Not only that, but you're on a mission. The only two people, or should I say beings, who you have to worry about impressing or making happy are up there," she said pointing to the sky.

It was decided that afternoon. I would submit the book as nonfiction. And the next day I sent out the queries—four by snail mail and eleven by email.

Agents being notoriously slow responders, I knew it could be a month or more before I heard from any of them. Then if they were interested in seeing my manuscript, it could be several months before they got around to reading it. I'd also read in a writer's magazine a few weeks earlier that there were online communities for aspiring authors. The article said that participants submitted the opening chapters of their works, and they were critiqued by other writers. The idea behind it was that writers could improve their books. Because nobody but Blanche had read a word of what I'd written, we decided to upload my first three chapters onto one of the sites. And after we did—the very second I hit that "submit" button—I felt like I'd left my baby all alone in a cold, dark, lonely place.

The site was run by Hall and Farnsworth, one of the world's biggest publishers. More than three thousand writers had submitted chapters. Many of them had considerable experience. More than a few had previously been published. I was a nobody. I had no experience or training. The moment I hit that button I felt like an idiot. Who was I kidding? I'd never written anything much longer than a grocery list in my entire life.

For the next three weeks, I checked the site every day. Five, ten, fifteen times I'd look. Each time there was nothing. Words can't describe how intimate I'd become with my story. And the deeper I got into the second draft, the more emotionally attached I became. A few times it got to a point where I had to get away from that computer. I felt like I was having a panic attack. My heart flipped a few beats, and I suddenly couldn't breath. I rushed to the front door, opened it, and had to gasp for air. I knew the whole thing was getting to me far more than it should have. I'd created in my mind a life and death scenario, and *The Real Ernest Hemingway* was in the center of it. The book had consumed me. Though that was all it was, just a book, it owned me. Twenty-four/seven it leaned on the back of my forehead, blurring everything else behind it. Tension was building. I couldn't wait to read the first review on the Hall and Farnsworth site. The anticipation was not only taking its toll on me mentally but physically as well. I was still able to sleep eight, nine hours a night, but I was always tired. Then one Friday after work, that long awaited first review finally appeared on my computer screen.

"Blanche!" I yelled from the bedroom. "Come here! It's here! The review's here!"

I couldn't help myself. I started reading it as she rushed from the kitchen. Then when she came into the room, she grabbed my shoulders from behind and peered at the screen with me. All I could say was, "Oh my God!"

Chapter 19

"What does it say? What does it say?" Blanche blurted, squeezing my shoulders as she shook them. "Come on, Jack!"

"I've only read half of it. Let me start from the beginning again."

I did, and my partner read along with me.

"I've been active on this site for three years now, and I must say this is far and away the best piece I have read. The senses of places you've painted with words are cinematic. I could see every one of them. As I read your words, I felt as if I were right alongside you and Ernest Hemingway. I felt the pain you both experienced at times. I smiled feeling the joy during the funny and happy parts. When you saw Hemingway appear at your side in front of his Key West home, so did I. When you were aboard the Pilar and that vicious storm came out of nowhere, I was on the deck with both of you—and just as stressed. And I, too, was relieved when the seas finally calmed and that light appeared.

I could go on and on, but I think I've made my point. When I read the last of your opening chapters, I was desperate to read more. And I will do just that when your captivating book is published. Do I believe that this is a nonfiction story? No, I can't say that I do. Nevertheless, from the very beginning it clenched the back of my neck, shoved my nose to its pages, and would not let go until I finished.

Thank you, Jack Phelan. I wish you all the best of luck with this."

Swiveling around in my chair, I looked at my wife. We were both beaming. Our smiles were so wide our cheeks swelled like two ecstatic cherubs. The goose bumps that had risen on my forearms as I read the review were still there. All the anxiety that weighed down my spirit for so long was gone.

I felt the small hope I'd fought so hard to keep alive swell and lift like a brightly-colored air balloon. I was rising higher and higher and looking down at all the doubts that had plagued me for months. They shrunk quickly until they became specks. Yes, the doubts were tiny at this joyful moment, but they'd never be totally gone. I had always been a tough-luck person. Nothing ever came easily. And whenever good things happened to me, they'd always felt like too little, too late. But this time was different. And I allowed myself to relish the wonderful news.

"Hot *damn!*" I said clenching my fists and giving them both one good hard jerk. "We did it, Blanche! We freaking did it!"

But that was only the beginning. I started getting one outstanding review after the next. And after just four weeks, *The Real Ernest Hemingway* was the number-one-ranked book on the Hall and Farnsworth site. Not only that but it stayed there. It finished in first place at the end of December and was then in contention for the site's "Book of the Year." I was riding high. I thought all along that I'd written something special. The reviews the book received only bolstered that belief.

Then there was even more good news.

Right after New Year's, I began hearing from the literary agents I'd contacted. And by the end of January I'd gotten responses from all but one. Ten agents in just one month wanted to see all or part of my manuscript—four of them in a single day. I couldn't believe it. I had gotten to know some very good writers on the website— authors who'd been trying to get published for years, and half of them never had a single agent willing to look at their works. I had ten. Though the recession was squeezing us tighter and tighter, Blanche and I didn't let it drag us down as much. Sure, I'd lost a few of my customers, and those small doubts about the book were still down on the ground eyeballing me, but I was almost positive that at least one agent would be getting back to me with good news.

Yes, things were looking up. And when Blanche and I awoke with the sun on Saturday, February 2nd, my forty-third birthday, we decided to take a ride up to Jonathon Dickinson State Park. Many times over the years we had gone there to stroll along the quiet nature trails and to discuss the good and bad going on in our lives. This time, unlike twenty years earlier when we'd gotten the devastating news that Blanche could never have children, it was all good. And so was the weather. It was one of those rare South Florida days when it was cool enough to put a little bounce in our steps. With both of us wearing hooded sweatshirts, we arrived at the park entrance just before it opened. There were no other visitors waiting to get in, and that was fine with us.

The narrow road was empty as we slowly drove through the miles of scattered pine trees and dense palmettos. Saying little, we scoured the surroundings for wildlife. And with the sun still low on the horizon, we were lucky enough to see three deer up close, one with small antlers. A couple of miles later, as we neared our favorite trail a mile before the road ends at the Loxahatchee River, Blanche pointed up ahead again.

In an excited whisper as if they might hear, she said, "Look . . . over there . . . a whole family of little piggies! There's the momma, the papa, and four babies."

I slowed down even more. And as we idled by them, the six black boars just kept on rooting along the grassy shoulder as if we didn't exist.

A few minutes later we parked on the side of the road. Side by side we started walking down a sandy trail. Not saying a whole lot, we listened to the calls of the blue jays and mockingbirds. We also heard the low-pitched, heart-broken call of a dove. As if it were in mourning, it hooted oo-wah-hoo-oo-oo!

"Sounds just like an owl, doesn't it?" I asked.

"Yes, it does."

We took a few more steps, and Blanche said, "This is an exciting time, Jack; isn't it? I mean with the book doing so well."

"Yup, it sure is. I just hope nothing ruins it. You know how things usually go for us. Just when it finally seems things might be getting better, POOF, everything seems to go all to hell again."

"Oh come on now," Blanche said turning to me as we continued to walk. "Don't start getting negative again. Think positive this time. You're always so pessimistic."

"You think I'm pessimistic? No, not really. I don't think so. *Realistic* . . . yes! I just can't be sure of anything until I've got it in my hands. But you know what? You're right. Let's not go there right now. Let's be happy this time."

As we continued to walk, my gaze lingered on my beautiful wife. Her high cheeks were rosy from the chilly air. Her flowing auburn hair hung in waves over her red sweatshirt to the belt loops of her jeans. With the denim snug against her hips, I thought for the thousandth time what a shame it was she couldn't have had kids. With her fine strong body, she was made to bear children. With her caring, unselfish mind, she would have made as good a mother as any woman on earth. Again I blew all that off. Putting my arm around her waist now, I said, "Damn right, hon. The book *is* going to make it."

"I know it's going to make it, Jack. Hey . . . ," she suddenly blurted as the smile on her face stretched wider, "who are we going to pick to produce the movie?"

"The movie? Come on. Get out of here."

"No, really! Why not? It could happen. It should happen. It's one fabulous story. I can see it on the marquis now, *The Real Ernest Hemingway!*"

"Yeah," I chimed playing the game now, "with Kevin Costner playing me."

"Perfect, he would be great. Who'd play Ernest?"

"I don't know. Who do you think?"

"How about Stacy Keach?"

"Done deal," I said with my arm still around her waist and giving her a squeeze. "He's perfect, too."

"Alright, we've got the two main characters. Who's going to be our producer? How about Martin Scorcese or Oliver Stone?"

"Now that's a tough choice. Oh geez . . . come on, we've got to stop this now. This is sick. We're like two kids playing make believe," I said loving every minute of it.

"Oh Jack," she said in a more serious tone now as she slid her arm around me, "I pray this all works out."

"I hope so."

"It will. I know it will. This book's going to be big. I'm not just saying that because you're my husband either. Some of those words are gilded with literary greatness."

"Gilded with literary greatness!" I said stopping in my tracks and stepping to the side. "And *I'm* supposed to be a writer? Maybe *you* missed your calling. Maybe *you* ought to pick up a pen and see what comes out of it."

Looking down at her pink and white sneakers and actually seeming a little embarrassed by the compliment, Blanche waved me off. "Oh stop. I'm no writer. I could never write an entire book."

"I wouldn't bet on it, kid. You ought to give it a crack sometime. Just try to write one good sentence. Then go from there. That's what Ernest told me."

"Who knows? Maybe someday."

After mulling the idea for a short moment she changed the subject. "Jack, how do you think he's doing?"

"Who?"

"Ernest."

"How bad *can* he be doing? He's up there," I said giving my head a little jerk upwards. "But you know what? I miss him. I really, really liked him."

With melancholic looks on our faces, we both looked up the trail now. Just forty yards from the end . . . it was almost time to turn back around.

"I've hoped he'd come back down, you know, pay me a short visit or something. But he hasn't."

"Think about it, Jack. I'm sure he would have had he been able to. But just as you told me, the only reason he came in the first place was to meet you. That and because it was the anniversary of his death."

"I know. But I still miss the guy."

Right then, the very second I said I missed Ernest, something strange happened, something very, very strange.

"Oh my God, Jack," Blanche blurted, "look at that!" And both of us froze mid-stride—still as stone statues.

Just ten yards in front of us something had come out of the trailside high grass. In all the years we'd been coming to the park, we'd never seen a bobcat. We'd always kept an eye out for them but never once saw one.

"He stopped right there . . ." I said in an excited whisper, "right in the middle of the trail.

One of the world's most elusive animals was looking at us. Instead of running off back into the palmettos, it was staring straight at us. It was an electrifying encounter yet at the same time subtle. Like most bobcats I'd seen in pictures, this one was brownish with black bars on its front legs. It also had the characteristic black tufts atop its pointy ears. But this one was different. This male was old, and it had a stocky body. And for some reason, the white around its mouth and chin put me to mind of Ernest's white moustache and beard.

"Arrr," it cried out in a surprisingly calm, friendly tone.

We could only stare at him.

Again, "Arrr."

Then, as if it had accomplished what it had intended, it slowly turned its head away and padded back into the brush.

"Jack . . . you don't think?"

Silently I rotated my head. Then in a low, reverent voice as if we'd just witnessed miracle, I slowly said, "I don't know, Blanche. I just don't know. After my time with Ernest, I believe anything is possible."

We talked about that cat for the rest of the weekend. We also talked about the future of my book. Enough time had passed since I'd queried the literary agents. Expecting my first response any day, I debated what I'd do if the first agent to get back happened to be one of my last choices. Would I contact all the others and tell them I had an offer? Should I give them a week or two to read the book and make up their minds? I didn't know what the proper etiquette was in the publishing industry. So I went to bed Sunday night thinking I'd go online soon as I got a chance. Maybe I could learn a thing or two about how things were done.

But none of that would be necessary. The very next day I heard back from the agent at the very top of my list. And she was one of New York's biggest.

Chapter 20

I had just walked in the door. Stinking of perspiration and grass clippings, I took off the wide-brimmed straw hat I always wore to work. As soon as I laid the goofy looking thing on the coffee table, Blanche came rushing in from the kitchen. She looked so excited I thought she'd burst. With both hands behind her back, she planted a good one on my lips then stepped back.

"Guess what came in the mail today," she said bobbing on her toes like a small child on Christmas morning.

It hadn't been a good day for me. I was tired, hot, and as always, filthy. Not only that but I'd lost two more accounts. When I answered Blanche, it was with as much enthusiasm as a condemned man heading for the gallows.

"I give up. What came in the mail?"

"A response letter from an agent!" she blurted whipping it around and wiggling the envelope in front of my eyes.

"And it's not from just any agent. It's from *thee* Sarah Roundhouse . . . your first choice."

"Uh oh," I said, taking it and holding it up to the late afternoon light coming in the side window. "I can't see anything. Guess I'd better open it."

Ripping an end off the envelope and pulling the letter out the side, I said, "Well, at least it's not one of those printed rejection cards they supposedly send most of the time."

This was it. Seven months it had taken to get to this point. I'd lived, slept, drank, ate, and breathed the book.

"I feel like we should have a drum roll or something," I said as I unfolded the white paper. Then I read it.

Dear Mr. Phelan, Thank you for giving me the opportunity to look at your work. While your idea does sound intriguing, I'm afraid I am not confident enough that The Real Ernest Hemingway is something that would appeal to the publishers with whom I presently work. Please keep in mind that my

decision is subjective. There may very well be other agents who will be very enthusiastic about your work. But, because I lack that enthusiasm, I'm afraid I'm going to have to pass. Sincerely,
Sarah Roundhouse.

To say I was devastated would be like calling the attack on Pearl Harbor somewhat disconcerting. Like an entire squadron of flaming Kamikazes, all my high hopes came crashing down on me at once.

"Blanche," I said slowly looking up from the letter to her eyes, "all that hard work! Two drafts, hundreds of hours racking my brain, a thousand spell checks, a thesaurus that's half worn out, all our bullshit dreams, even the four days with Hemingway . . . where the fuck did any of it get me?"

"Oh come on, Jack, don't curse like that. It's not the end, honey. It's just the beginning. Maybe not the beginning we'd hoped for but just the beginning all the same. Sarah Roundhouse isn't the only agent selling books in New York. She's not the final say to anything. You're still a million miles from failing. Come on now!"

"Yeah, yeah," I said with my head slung low. "Just let me go, hon. I want to take a shower."

"Go ahead. I'll have a nice, cold beer waiting for you."

Already slogging my way to the bathroom by now, I said over my shoulder, "You better have a twelve pack."

I didn't drink a twelve pack that night but came pretty close. We sat on the porch till well after dark, and the whole time Blanche tried to sooth my wrecked spirit. All her consoling, along with the beer, did eventually dull some of my disappointment but certainly not all of it. There was now a depressing dark frame surrounding my every thought. What little hope I had left was jammed somewhere in it, too, but it was so overshadowed by worry it was barely discernible.

That first rejection was the beginning of a trend. Sarah Roundhouse would not be the last agent to reject my book. The next three nixed it as well. All of them came in the mail that same week, and each felt like a bucket of cold water had been heaved on my smoldering dreams. My inner fire was all but out.

For the rest of that week and the following weekend, a deep concern filled the mental void left by those vanishing hopes. I didn't mention it to Blanche. "What if, just what if I fail with this book?" I asked myself. "Will He end me? Will I get into some kind of fatal accident or simply fade into thin air? Is that all this book thing is, one final chance?"

The uncertainty was maddening. All week long while on my rider mower, those doomsday thoughts sapped my energy and numbed my senses. On Thursday I lost yet another account, and on Friday Blanche came home with more wonderful news. She told me her bosses might have to let her go. They, too, were losing accounts. It wasn't definite, but the best case scenario was they'd have to shave even more hours from her work schedule. When I read the paper before going to work each morning, I'd fume. Everything around me seemed to be collapsing. Prices of everything from potatoes to gasoline to new cars were going through the roof. Our vehicles were getting old and tired. I felt down-in-the-dirt defeated. For the first time in my life, crime was beginning to look like a viable option.

I started thinking about stealing. I was sick and tired of watching Blanche and me go down, down, down. It didn't even matter that I now knew there was such a thing as life after death. I'd never believed in it before I went into that coma, yet my entire adult life I'd still walked the straight and narrow. But things were different now. Something needed to be done. Blanche and I had always played by the rules— jumped through all the necessary hoops—and for what? To end up where we were? Nuh, uh, I thought. That's not going to happen. I've got to do something.

Chapter 21

Blanche continued to look for a full-time job, but her efforts were fruitless. I'd gone online looking for part-time work myself, but that was just as hopeless. The whole country was in a deep recession. And Florida was buried at the bottom of it. Every time I searched job sites, it was always the same tired story. All I seemed to be qualified for were eight-dollar-an-hour jobs at big-box stores or fast food joints. There was no way that was going to happen. I wasn't about to sell an hour of my lifetime for a paltry six dollars and fifty cents after taxes. I refused to trade two hours labor for three measly gallons of gasoline. I would not work one fourth of a day just to drive my pickup truck fifty miles.

Driving to and from work each day, I felt my fear building. I noticed the lines in front of the food bank were getting longer and longer. But there was something else going on that scared me even more than the bread lines. Each time I passed one of the three banks along the way, I began to eyeball them. And every time I went by the gun shop, I turned my head as well.

One minute I'd tell myself I was crazy and the next I'd be thinking about driving around one of the banks to see if it had a back entrance. I wondered what would be the best time of day to do the unthinkable act I was contemplating. I kept scoping out the banks more and more closely while driving by. I tried to see if I could learn the timetable of the armored cars. If I were going to do this thing—risk everything, possibly take a bullet to the head or wind up behind steel bars-- I wanted to be damned sure the gamble would be profitable. Sometimes seconds after thinking that way, I'd shake my head as if listening for loose screws. Other times I'd slap the side of my head and try to bring myself back to reality. Yes, the thoughts I was entertaining scared the hell out of me. Was I crazy? What was I going to do if I did pull a robbery off? Rush home? Tell Blanche I just robbed a bank? Tell her to get into the car—we're heading to Mexico? Insane as it all was, it seemed more and more like a viable option. Then by the end of February, things grew even bleaker.

Luberdorf and Ackerly took away Blanche's Wednesdays. She was now working only four mornings. I lost more lawn accounts. A third of my business was gone. On top of that, twelve of my queries had been rejected. There were only three more out there. And at lunchtime on a Tuesday, I parked my truck and trailer full of lawn equipment behind Ron's Gun Shop.

"Can I help you?" asked the stocky, camouflage-clad man behind the counter.

"I just wanted to poke around a little. Get an idea what 45's are selling for."

"They're over here," the unshaven guy said as he side-stepped along the glass display counter.

"Did you have anything special in mind?"

"No. Not really," I said studying the pistols beneath the glass. "I was looking for something inexpensive. Just wanted to see what price they started at."

"Well, I've got Colts, Berettas, Glocks and all the rest, but this one here is the cheapest."

He took it out of the case and handed it to me. As I looked it over, he did the same thing to me. It were as if he were very suspicious, like he was making a mental sketch of my face. That's how I took it at least. And as I handled the gun, my hands began to perspire.

"What do you plan to use it for?"

Oh shit, I thought, *he's got my number. He sees me come in here all sweaty and dirty and figures I'm some kind of lowlife.*

"Oh," I said, forcing my eyes to meet his, "I just thought it wouldn't be a bad idea to have a little something in the house. You know . . . *protection.*"

Still looking at me, he just nodded as if to say, *Yupper, sure, heard that one before. You come in here looking for the cheapest thing you can get. Yeah huh!*

A few more uncomfortable moments later I said, "You know what? I think I'll take this one. This and the smallest box of ammo you have. You take credit cards of course."

"Whooah!" he said sniggering deeply. "You can't just walk out of here with a handgun. There's a three-day waiting period in Florida."

Oh shit, I'm going to have to come back? I thought but said, "That's right . . . of course! We might as well fill out the paperwork right now then. I'll leave you a deposit."

Relieved as I was when I finally got out of that place, I still had to go back after seventy-two hours. Looking at my watch as I walked to my truck, I saw that it said 1:30. I figured I'd wait until after work on Friday so I wouldn't look all that eager. That would be sometime around 4:30.

After leaving the gun shop, I passed the turnoff to Saint Robert's Catholic Church. I was so torn. Except for a few weddings and both my parents' funerals, I hadn't planted a foot inside a church since I was seventeen. Just a kid back then, I was running around with all kinds of girls. I was also doing other things that were clearly beyond the forbidden border between mischief and unadulterated trouble. Anyway, after I'd confessed my sins in a dark booth, the priest balled me out and told me I'd been living the life of a pagan. Since that happened, I always thought the man of the cloth had been far too hard on me, so I'd never gone back into a church on my own volition.

But driving down Poinciana Boulevard now, I was thinking about it now. Should I go into Saint Robert's, throw myself down on my knees, and ask God for forgiveness, guidance, and help? Yes, I probably should have. But I didn't. With my mind pulling itself in a dozen directions I went back to work and climbed onto my rider. I couldn't think straight. Yet that's all I did—think. And more than once I found myself riding over a swath of grass I'd already cut. I just wanted to scream.

Chapter 22

When I got home late that afternoon, things didn't get any better. Blanche hesitantly greeted me with yet another rejection letter. It wasn't really a letter, just one of those impersonal notices printed on a card. Like most of the other generic rejections I'd received, the agent's signature was stamped on not signed. Now there were only two others still out there.

I moped around the house all evening, but my mind certainly wasn't sluggish. It was all hopped up. Thoughts were still bouncing around in every direction at once—none of them good. I couldn't rationally think through any of my dark fears or clandestine plans. Only fragments of each thought appeared, yet all of them were entangled. All I could decipher were the loose ends. I'd planned on working out some kind of strategy for my heist but couldn't. All those fractured thoughts just kept stampeding in and out of my consciousness. They were all a blur. Fear, guilt, our financial mess, Ernest, Blanche, prison bars, potential gunshots, heaven, hell, the failing manuscript—all of it and more were like a hundred sandbags weighing heavily on my shoulders. And they were breaking me. I was in a state of near maddening confusion.

Blanche didn't look good either. My dark mood was getting to her. All I did was sit alongside her in my recliner and stare at the television, seeing none of it. By the time Jeopardy was just about over and I hadn't answered a single clue, Blanche had had it.

"Come on, Jack. For God's sake, pull yourself together. You look miserable. Fuck that rejection. It's not the end of the world."

I could not believe my ears. Since the day I met her, I'd only heard her use that word twice.

"It's not just the damned rejection," I came back. "It's everything else as well."

Then I slipped saying, "There's a lot more on my mind than you realize."

"A lot more than I realize? Exactly what is that supposed to mean? What are you talking about here?"

She'd muted the TV, raised herself from her recliner's backrest and was staring over the lamp table between us. Looking back at her tired face, I squirmed in my chair. "Nothing," I lied, "nothing. It's just the same old worries getting to me."

Then a way to take her attention from what I'd just said popped into my head. And it wasn't a lie—a diversion surely but not a lie.

"Okay, you want to know what's getting to me? On top of everything else, I'm worried about what'll happen if the book fails . . . if it never gets published." Pointing up toward the ceiling fan now, I went on, "What is He up there going to do? Just let me go on living my life? Or will He end it because I failed? That's something to think about, Blanche. That's a damned serious thing to worry about."

"Oh stop. He's not *cruel*. He's not just going to take you away," she said in a voice that suddenly didn't seem quite as confident.

"See, I told you. It *is* something to worry about."

"No it's not," she said leaning back in her chair again and looking at the TV but not paying attention to it.

A few moments of uncomfortable silence later she rolled her weary head in my direction again. Though she'd been carrying her own share of debilitating mental baggage, she said, "Jack, it'll all work out. You'll see. You've only sent out fifteen queries. There are hundreds of literary agents. You've only scratched the surface."

"Look, I appreciate your sympathy and optimism, hon. But even if it does *someday* get published, how are we supposed to live in the meantime? Along with everything else we still owe more than eight thousand from when I was in the hospital. We're in serious debt. Something has to be done, soon. We need to get a hold of some money . . . now."

"I've told you. We'll just keep making small payments to the hospital and the minimum on the credit cards. We'll get out of this mess eventually."

"Sorry, I don't want to wait for eventually."

"Well," she said throwing her hands up as if surrendering, "we don't have a choice. All we can do is keep paying a little at a time."

"Hmmmph, a little at a time until we're eighty years old— *if I'm still around.*"

"Would you please stop thinking that way? You're going to be around for a long, long time."

"I'm glad you're so sure."

Then loosening some of the tenseness in my voice, I said, "You know, Blanche, when I was with Ernest he told me that being a man is a tough business. And he was one hundred percent right. But tough as it is, he didn't know a whole lot about not having money. Other than when he first lived in Paris, he never had financial clouds hunkered over his head and spirit. He was never a working man in this screwed up, twenty-first century. In many respects, he had it made. And it was still difficult being a man. Now . . . today, forget about it. Things are ten times harder."

"I hear you."Blanche said. "But what about being a woman today?"

"That's another can of worms. Let's not even bother opening that one right now. I don't know how women with families and jobs keep the pace they do. I've got all I can do to take care of myself . . . to take care of us."

Nothing was solved that night. And when I awoke the next morning, my dreary anxiety was still there. It didn't get any better as the day wore on either. And by the time Thursday dragged itself around, everything was coming to a head. I was like a swollen red carbuncle filled with poison and about to burst. I was at the end of my frayed rope.

I worked through lunch so I'd have time to drive by the banks again. I'd pretty much decided to hit the Palm Federal Credit Union on Poinciana Boulevard. I didn't like that it was situated on one of West Palm Beach's busiest thoroughfares, but if I were going to do this thing and by some chance possibly get away with it, I wanted some real money. I could have gone way out west where it was a lot less populated. But I knew the carrot at the end of the stick would be much smaller. I'd also decided that if I got away with it, I would not mention a thing to Blanche. I'd simply stash the money somewhere and take small amounts at a time. I'd simply tell her I'd been doing a little extra work on the side.

Yeah, I'd figured that much out alright. But I was still trying to talk myself out of the whole desperate, reckless idea. Certainly I was no big-time desperado, but that did nothing to stop my mental tug-of-war. All that morning my mind flooded with thoughts.

Are you out of your tree? Bank robbery? Shit, man, get a grip on yourself. You are not holding up a freaking bank. Forget yourself, for God's sake. You could end up killing somebody else—somebody who's in there just trying to make half a living. Oh no, I'm not going to do it, huh? Just watch! I am going to do this thing. I've got to. There's no other way. I'm sick and damned tired of fighting my way up shit's creek with a battered paddle. It's a done deal!

Over and over and back and forth, I tortured myself. With the evil side still winning, I worked through lunch so I could knock off early and take one last look at Palm Federal. I knew I really should go inside the place and poke around to scope it out. I sure didn't want any surprises when I went busting in there. But I didn't go inside. The last thing I needed was to be filmed by the bank's video cameras before I absolutely had to.

My plan was pretty much worked out. After picking up the pistol the next day, I'd lie low for a couple of weeks. Knowing that police investigators would check all recent, local gun sales, I decided I'd slip a white sock over the 45 when it came time to do the deed. I'd put on loose-fitting clothes to keep my body type somewhat anonymous and wear something bulky beneath my shirt to make myself look like a suicide bomber. There would be a ball cap on my head and a mask over my face. I wouldn't utter a single word. All I'd do is hand over a note that said I was wired to explosives and what I wanted.

But even before I'd walk into the bank, there was something else that needed to be done. I'd call in a bogus bomb scare to the police. I'd tell them it was planted inside a hotel on the other side of town. Surely that would divert most of their cruisers. I'd immediately split from the pay phone, wait about five minutes, then enact my plan. Walking off the street and up to the bank's entrance, my head would be low so the outside cameras couldn't get a good shot of me. My pickup and trailer would be parked on a nearby side street I'd already scoped out.

After finishing my last lawn at 3:15 that day, I headed to the bank. I felt my face grimace as I passed by Ron's Gun Shop, and two blocks later with my mind all jammed up the way it was, I almost rear-ended a mail truck stopped at a red light. It was as if I were hearing somebody else's voice when I blurted to myself, "Man, pull yourself together!"

Driving very slowly by the front and side of the bank, I looked really hard to see inside the windows again. No guard—but that was no guarantee. There could easily be a retired police or military marksman sitting or standing in there just waiting for some joker like me to come along.

Still idling up the side street, just beyond the bank's back parking lot and stone wall, I glanced at the houses around me. It was an old neighborhood. The street was quiet and lined on both sides by unusually tall trees for this part of Florida. All the small block homes had driveways. There were virtually no cars parked on the street. I'd have no problem finding a parking spot long enough to accommodate the truck and trailer.

I swung around a few blocks and came back out onto Poinciana Boulevard. This time I made a left to head home. Tense as an accused murderer just before the judge reads his verdict, I tried to concentrate on my driving. With my palms and everything else sweating, I steered the best I could along the busy thoroughfare.

About two miles up the business-to-business corridor, on the corner of yet another block full of huge competing signs, a small one caught my eye. It was one of those fluorescent green cardboard deals stapled to a wooden electric pole. The printing on it read:

Big Bazaar

Friday and Saturday

Saint Robert's Catholic Church

Beneath the message there was an arrow pointing to the right. Sure, I well knew all along where Saint Robert's was. But for some reason my eyes were pulled toward that one tiny sign amongst all the other huge eyesores. That seemed odd— no, uncanny. Was it guidance from Him above? Was it intended to get me to that church? Did Ernest have something to do with it? For the few short seconds before I reached that corner of the block, I fought with myself.

Should I turn? Should I go to the church, drop to my knees and pray? Pray to God to heal my sick mind? Yeah, I'm going to do it. No, it was just a cardboard sign. I'm not going. Yes, I am. No, I'm . . . .

Chapter 23

I don't know what made me decide do it, but at the very last fraction of a second, I swung the steering wheel—hard and to the right. All the equipment in the secondhand, unenclosed trailer I'd recently bought, except for the riding mower, shifted. The two walk-behind mowers, both edgers, my water cooler—all of it shifted hard and slammed into the trailer's steel side rail. Then the whole thing fishtailed behind me. It was a few, long seconds before I got the truck and trailer under control again. And the instant I did, I blurted, "Dammit, Ernest! Is that you! You don't have to play so freaking rough!" The words had barely jumped from my mouth when I realized that if it were Ernest, he wasn't playing at all. He was plenty serious.

A few minutes later I trudged up the church's front steps feeling like I was being pulled up them. It was an old church, and as the heavy wooden door closed behind me, the creaking hinges seemed to desecrate the quiet. There was no vestibule inside the entrance. I stepped right into the dark nave, dipped my fingertips in holy water, and slowly genuflected. The gesture felt alien. It had been a long time since I'd done it.

Standing there for a moment, I looked around in the dusky light. It was old alright, the kind of place webs draping from the ceilings and corners would be expected. Dust particles floated in the dim light of the faded stained-glass windows. Beneath them, the fourteen Stations of the Cross were evenly spaced on the two side walls. The rows of dark wooden pews were tight, and the Missals lying in them were black and worn. The place even smelled old, yet somehow that only enhanced the feeling that I was in the holy presence of God.

Only one other person was in the church. From the back it looked like a woman praying at the altar. After taking it all in, I stepped into the last pew and I fell to my knees.

Slowly, I made the sign of the cross a second time. Then I lowered my head and muttered beneath my breath, "Good God

. . . why? Why did you allow me to come back? Why would you want me to write a book that nobody wants? Not a single agent has showed a sign of interest. And Lord, why do Blanche and I have to struggle the way we do? We don't want much. I'm living in a place I've come to hate. There are so many other places I'd rather be. I've accepted that for now, and I'm making the best of it. But my best doesn't seem good enough. Things get harder and harder. For the first time ever, we've fallen behind on our bills. God, all we want is enough to get by. We've always driven old, used cars. I live in tee shirts and jeans. The sneakers on my feet are cheap. At home we tear paper towels in half. We add water to make our mustard and ketchup last longer."

Pausing now, I raised my eyes to the distant altar. The suffering Jesus hanging on the cross was blurred. I sniffled twice then wiped my eyes.

"I'm coming so close to doing something, Lord. Something I don't want to do. But I need the money. Please help me. Can you send me some assurance? Some kind of sign telling me that if I don't commit the evil act I have in mind, things will still work out? I am so mentally weak right now. Please . . . please help me!"

I was so deep into my plea that I hadn't noticed that the woman at the altar was now walking up the center aisle. Her gait was slow and unsteady, and her head was down. As she stepped closer, I saw that her clothes were old. There was a dark kerchief on her bowed head, and the long, plain cotton dress she wore was tattered. Still facing the cross, I watched her approach from the corners of my eyes.

Just before she walked by me, I saw her raise her head. I allowed mine to turn toward her. I hoped that in the cathedral's silence she hadn't heard me gasp at the sight of her face. If she did, she didn't show it. She only smiled.

Gracing my eyes was one of the most beautiful young women I'd ever seen. But at the same time she was ghastly. With a lock of golden hair hanging from beneath her kerchief, she had the face of a teenaged angel. Her hope-filled, gray eyes seemed to brighten up the church the same way her smile did her face. But there was something on her face that ruined it all. It was far from pretty. It was on the left side and hung from her jawbone. It was a growth and the most unsightly thing I had ever seen. Like a stretched blue balloon filled with liquid, it dangled, bounced and swayed as she walked. Probably four inches in length, it brushed back and forth over her collarbone.

I managed to smile back at her and to hold that smile until she walked by. Then I turned my head and looked back up at the cross. I stared at it as the aged door behind me creaked closed. Then I dropped my head and began to pray again. I no longer asked God for *things*. I just kept repeating over and over the only three prayers I remembered.

I don't know how long I remained in that church. It had to be close to an hour. But I do know that when I finally finished praying, I slowly lifted my eyes back to the cross, rose to my feet, and said, "Thank you. Thank you so very much."

Then I walked out.

Although I'd be late getting home to Blanche, I now knew I had to make one more stop. Driving from the church back up to Poinciana Boulevard, I turned right and headed straight for Ron's Gun Shop.

When I entered the store there was a different clerk standing behind the counter. I told the thin, older man that I wanted to cancel my order. He was far from enthused, but that was fine. I couldn't care in the least. I'd finally been freed from the insane plan that had obsessed and tormented me for so long.

When I got home Blanche looked both worried and relieved.

"Geez, Jack, where were you? You're never this late," she said looking at her watch. "It's twenty after six."

At first I didn't say a thing. I just gave her a big wide smile, reached out, grabbed her by the shoulders and planted a really good one on her lips. Then I said, "Sorry. There were a few things I *had* to do. Next time I'll call. I would have, but I didn't realize it was getting so late."

"Well, what did you have to do?"

Looking deep into her green eyes and holding them with my own, I said, "Honey, I had to do a couple of things. Can we just leave it at that?"

Searching my face in silence, she slowly nodded her head. Then after a long moment, a small, trusting smile rose on her face, and she said, "Sure, Jacky . . . why not? We can leave it at that."

Then reaching in the back pocket of her denim shorts, she pulled out a folded letter. She looked so very disappointed. Clenching the letter with both hands in front of her now, she said in a solemn tone, "This came in the mail today. I'm sorry, but I opened it."

I didn't take the letter right away. I just stood there looking at the downcast look on my wife's face. It dug into me at first. But then something happened. Somehow her eyes seemed to betray her expression. And just as that red flag popped up in my mind, those eyes widened. Then in the time it takes to snap a finger, they lit up as if she'd just won the Powerball Jackpot. Suddenly smiling wider than I'd seen her in years, she flung her hands toward the ceiling, shook the letter as if it were a million dollar check, and screamed, "JACK . . . YOU DID IT! IT'S FROM AN AGENT! HE WANTS TO SEE YOUR ENTIRE MANUSCRIPT!"

She threw her arms around me and started jumping up and down like a kid who'd just gotten permission to go to summer camp. "You did it! You did it! You did it!" she said. "Here, take a look. It's from the Bernard Sheehan Agency. Didn't you say they were one of the biggest?"

"Yeah, I sure did."

Slowly I read it aloud, "Dear Mister Phelan, after reading your query letter and the first three chapters of *The Real Ernest Hemingway*, I must say that I am quite enthusiastic about it. If you will, please send me the entire manuscript in an email attachment. I will be glad to read it in its entirety. Though it normally takes up to three months for me to get back to an author, I am very impressed with your story and want to expedite the process. I begin my vacation next

Saturday, March 10th and will have sufficient time to read your work. I should be able to get back to you shortly after I return to my office on the 26th. Sincerely, Amber Rinaldi."

"Oh Jack, isn't that great news?"

"You bet it is. Give me another hug."

And she did. Then we opened a bottle of champagne we'd been saving. Shortly after I'd sent out the query letters, Blanche had bought it at the grocery store and was saving it for just such an occasion. I can't tell you how many times I'd opened the refrigerator door and grunted when I saw that green bottle lying on its side in there. I thought we'd never open it.

We celebrated on the porch that night and of course, our spirits were high. But mine weren't as lofty as Blanche's. Sure, with the return of my sanity and the reincarnation of my hopes, I felt really good. But true to my usual form, I had reservations. I didn't tell Blanche, but I had hoped to hear back from Bernard Sheehan himself. He's one of the heavyweight agents in New York, not Amber Rinaldi. I'd never heard of her before.

Right away I started thinking, *Amber . . . with a name like that she's got to be quite young. What is she, some kind of agent trainee? Did Bernard Sheehan simply look at my letter and hand it and the three chapters to this Amber? Not only that, but hadn't all those other agents already read at least part of my story? None of them took it! Who says it's going to be any different this time?*

Before going to bed that night, I went online to the agency's site. As I suspected, there was a bit there about Amber Rinaldi. She was far and away the youngest agent. Though she'd graduated from Cornell and had three years editing experience with a publisher, she'd only been an agent for a year. And there was something else that bothered me. It also said that she was actively seeking new writers for her list. Reading between the lines again, I figured she couldn't have been around long enough to have built solid relationships with any publishers.

Nevertheless, as we lay in the darkness of our bedroom that night, I felt much better about myself. I had done the right things that afternoon, and now we had some hope again. Enough hope that just before I dozed off, I whispered under my breath, "Don't worry, Ernest. I won't let you down."

Chapter 24

The next two weeks were quite uneventful, and that was fine. We didn't get any deeper in debt. I didn't lose any more accounts. And I darn well appreciated having my sanity back. The possibility of hearing good news from Amber kept me going as well. She had said she'd be returning to work on Monday the 26th, and I was counting the days. Every evening while checking my emails, I crossed another day off the Defenders of Wildlife calendar tacked to the wall.

I'd always been an early riser, getting up and about by six o'clock. But when the big day finally lumbered around, I had coffee brewing by four. I'd woken up to go to the bathroom, and there was no way I was getting back to sleep. Perpetually the over-thinker, I always have been one to twist, turn, flip and flop every thought. The anticipation was just too much. I couldn't wait to hear from Amber.

When I went to work, the rest of the morning crawled as slowly as a last-legs tortoise. And the afternoon didn't move any faster. Constantly checking my watch and swearing it had died on my wrist, I just couldn't wait to get home and find out if Amber had called.

"Blanche!" I called out when I finally did come through the door, "Yo . . . where are you?"

Flinging my straw hat onto the sofa as if it were a Frisbee, I noticed my dirty, sorry condition in the wall mirror. I could only shake my head as I headed for the kitchen.

"There you are." I said as Blanche came through the glass sliders from the backyard.

"Oh . . . hi, hon! I had to bring these sheets in from the clothesline."

"Forget the sheets," I said after giving her a quick peck, "Did she call?"

"No. Not yet. She probably figures you've been at work. I'm sure she will soon."

"Oh, damn, that's not a good sign," I said, going to the refrigerator for a beer. "I've been going out of my head all day long."

"I'll bet you have. Come on now. Let's go into the living room. I'll get a glass of wine and a beer."

I drank three cans of beer—no call. We ate dinner in the recliners while watching TV—still no call. We went to bed at nine, and that ray of hope had again dimmed. I was devastated. This made no sense. She specifically said she'd call after returning to her office on the 26th. I'd taken the "after" to mean that very day. For two hours I couldn't fall asleep. I rolled from side to side trying to decipher exactly what she'd meant. And no matter how I looked at it, I was not happy.

By Tuesday night I was very, very disappointed. By Wednesday, I was damned angry. By Thursday I had a full-blown case of what Ernest called the black ass. But early Friday evening while working on my first beer, the telephone finally rang.

Blanche and I gave each other a wide-eyed, could-that-be-her look. I took one deep breath, let it out, and picked the wireless from the table between our chairs.

As if I'd been doing nothing but meditating for the past three torturous weeks, I calmly said, "Hello," as if it were a question.

"Hello!" said the cheery young voice on the other end. "Can I please speak to Jack Phelan?"

"This is Jack," I said.

"Jack, this is Amber Rinaldi from the Bernard Sheehan Literary Agency. How are you today?"

"I'm doing just fine. It's good to hear from you . . . I hope."

She chuckled then said, "I'm so sorry I couldn't get back to you earlier. I planned on calling you Monday but didn't get back to the office until today. Somebody very close to me passed away and . . . well, I think you know how that goes."

"Sure I do. I'm very sorry about your loss."

"Thank you. I appreciate that."

A short moment passed, but then she continued, "Okay . . . let's get down to business now. First I want to tell you that I absolutely loved reading *The Real Ernest Hemingway*. Mister Sheehan has read it as well, and he, too, is very impressed with it. So, after talking it over, we've decided we would like our agency to represent you. If you will agree with the terms of our contract, I will do everything I can to make sure your book is published. We think it could have enormous potential."

With the phone to my ear, I nodded at Blanche. Excitedly shaking her small fists, her eyes welled up with tears. They weren't just tears of joy but tears also fueled by an immense sense of relief. She wanted to scream at the top of her lungs. As I smiled at her, my vision became blurry. Being the hopelessly emotional sot I am, I felt like I was about to implode. One breath away from breaking down, I turned my head away from Blanche and managed to hold onto my composure.

"I would be thrilled to work with you, Amber," I said. "Thank you. Thank you so very much."

Amber went on to say that she and Mister Sheehan weren't exactly sure how publishers or the reading public might react to my book being categorized as nonfiction. But she also said she and Mr. Sheehan were willing to take a chance. She told me that since they'd both found every single passage so moving and believable, listing it the way I wanted to, as nonfiction just could turn out to be a huge selling point. And that was another relief. I didn't have to tell her that I would never have agreed to categorize it as fiction.

Two days later the contract arrived in the mail. From the research I'd previously done, it seemed as if all the usual stipulations were in it. The agency would get fifteen percent of domestic sales—twenty for foreign. Not once, not twice, but three times Blanche made me read one particular part of the contract aloud. There was something in there concerning potential film rights. And boy did that one get us going. We had a great time fantasizing about that possibility.

The next morning I signed the contract and hustled it right down to the post office. I even sprang for the extra money to send it registered mail. From then on, every day felt like Christmas to Blanche and me. And after we put out the bedroom light every night, I shared my joy with Ernest Hemingway. I also thanked God.

Exactly two weeks from the day Amber had called with the good news, Blanche and I got yet another surprise. South Florida had been going through a dry spell for more than a week, and our lawn was looking rough. Brown spots the shade of old doormats were spreading quickly. So one night right after the sun had gone down, Blanche went out front to turn on the sprinkler for a while. We'd just finished dinner in the recliners and were getting ready to watch a *Cheers* rerun. I went into the kitchen and rinsed off our plates, and just as I finished and turned off the faucet, I heard a scream. It was long and guttural, starting off as a shrill and quickly evolving into a full blown scream.

"HIYEEEEEAAAAAAAAAAA!"

Oh my good God! I thought she must have gotten hit by a car. Talk about blood curdling; this one froze still the blood in my veins. My heart literally stopped, missed a beat, hesitated, and then finally turned over again.

I bolted out of the kitchen, through the living room, and toward the front door. But before I got there, she screamed again, "OHHH MYYY GOD! JAAAAAACK! COME QUICK! HURRY! I BROKE MY LEG!"

Charging outside, I ran to where she was laying on her back and dropped knees first to the grass.

"Oh, Jack," she cried, "I broke my leg or my ankle."

"Calm down, honey," I said stroking her damp hair as the oscillating sprinkler showered us with water. "Maybe you just sprained your ankle."

With the excruciating pain rushing her desperate frightened words out, she said, "NO! NO! It isn't sprained! I heard my bone crack! I think it's my ankle! I stepped into that little hole we've been meaning to fill up and twisted it!

146

When I went down, my foot was stuck in the hole! I heard it crack! Oh my God, call an ambulance. Hurry!"

She was wearing shorts and flip flops, and in the dim light I saw a bulge on her ankle the size of a small cantaloupe. Gently I touched it with my finger tips. It was nasty. As the sprinkler doused us with water another time, I said, "Honey, maybe you just sprained it. Come on. Let me help you inside. We'll put some ice on it."

"Godammit, Jack, NOOO! IT'S BROKEN! Please, just get me to the hospital!"

I grabbed her under the arms and lifted her up. She put her arm around my shoulders, and I helped her slowly, painfully hop to her Hyundai Elantra. With both of us soaking wet by now and with dead grass and sand all over Blanche's back and in her hair, I sped off to Palm Beach General.

"God, oh God, why did this have to happen, Jack? The pain is killing me. I don't know how much longer I can take it."

Lord, how I wished I could take her suffering for her. Looking at her alongside me, I gritted my teeth so hard they should have broken. She was slumped against the door with her head leaning against the window. It was getting dark by now, and as we tore past a streetlight, its somber glow flashed through the windshield and over her face. I could see all her deep pain scrunched up in it.

"Son of a bitch!" I blurted slamming my fist on the top of the dashboard. "WHY? WHY didn't I fill that fucking hole? I am so sorry, honey."

With pain lacing her words, she said in a weak, scared tone, "It's not your fault, Jack. We've both twisted our ankles in that thing a few times. I was going to fill it myself but kept forgetting about it, too."

"I meant to do it last weekend when I went out to cut the grass," I said swinging a hard left into the hospital parking lot. "I was going to fill the damned thing when I finished the lawn. Shit, it isn't even a hole—just a three inch depression."

I slammed to a stop in front of the emergency entrance and raced inside. Two nurses rushed back outside with me, and we carefully loaded Blanche into a wheelchair. It was just after eight o'clock when they took Blanche into a small room adjacent to the Friday-night-crowded waiting area. Sitting upright in a chair alongside the bed and stroking the back of her hand, I watched as a nurse asked Blanche questions; then took her pulse and blood pressure. When she was finished, the pert redhead elevated the back of the bed so that Blanche was almost sitting up. She put an ice pack on her ankle and asked, "On a scale of one to ten, how bad is the pain" Blanche told her it was a ten, and then the nurse was gone.

About every thirty minutes for the next two hours, that nurse or another poked her head into the doorway and asked how she was doing. Each time Blanche said, "Not good," and again the nurse would disappear.

By a quarter to ten, I was pissed. Still no doctor had come. I knew that a break like Blanche's was something that couldn't be taken lightly. I'd heard that blood clots could form and actually endanger a person's life. My wife's ankle and now her foot were swollen and red. As unsightly as they were, things then got downright ugly. For years Blanche had occasionally gotten bad cramps in her feet—not all that often, maybe every three or four months. And they were always short lived, usually lasting only about a minute. But they were very painful. And now, of all the times for it to happen, she felt one coming on.

"Oh shit, Jack," she said, "I feel a cramp coming on."

"Oh no, don't say that. Not now."

"I feel it. It hurts. Good Lord, please no. Not now. Owww! Ow, ow, ow! Look at them. Look at my toes!"

Red as they'd been, they were now turning crimson. Her ankle was badly shattered—not broken—but shattered. Her toes clenched tighter and tighter, and they got even redder. All the joints were turning white. And as if someone had tightened a vice on her excruciating ankle, Blanche let out a scream that made the ones on the lawn sound like whispers.

"AAAHHHH!   AAAHHHHHHH!! AHHHHHHHHHHHH!!! HELP MEEEEEE! I WANT TO DIEEE!"

I thought that one of those blood clots just might have formed in one of her veins or arteries. It entered my mind that a clot could be coursing her circulatory system—about to lodge somewhere and possibly obstruct her blood flow. Suddenly, like a low black cloud from hell, an eerie sense of impending doom darkened the stark white room. The ugly haunting possibility that my Blanche could be dying right there, right then, right in front of my eyes mortified me.

"Oh shit! Hold on, honey. I'll be right back! I'll get some help."

But I didn't have to. Two nurses and a doctor came running through the doorway.

"AAAHHHHHOOOOWWWWW!!!!!"

"What's wrong?" the doctor asked pulling the ice pack off.

"What's wrong is that she's in *fucking* agony. *Godammit*, what's wrong with you idiots? We're here over two hours, and nobody has done shit. For Christ's sake take care of my wife!"

"Alright, alright, calm down," the doctor said to me. Then to Blanche he said, "You're going to be okay. Just hold on a few seconds. We're going to give you morphine."

She bit down hard on her lip and squirmed in agony as the nurses jammed huge hypodermics into both her arms. Her face was scarlet now and every bit as contorted as her toes. I'd never in my life seen anybody suffer like this. No living thing—man nor beast—should ever have to endure such agony.

Thankfully the morphine took only seconds to kick in. Once it did, Blanche calmed down somewhat, and they wheeled her to the X-ray room.

Chapter 25

The doctor who was to perform surgery the next day later told me it was one of the worst breaks he'd ever seen. After that they monkeyed around with all kinds of tests, and it wasn't until 12:30 a.m. that they finally took my battered wife up to a room. Because the doctor told me Blanche would be sleeping and there was nothing I could do, I went out to the dark, deserted parking lot and drove home. When I got there, puddles the size of Lake Michigan were all over the front lawn. The sprinkler was still going. Like a zombie I walked through its spray and turned off the spigot at the side of the house. Then I went inside to our empty bedroom and hugged Blanche's pillow until I fell asleep.

At ten the next morning, I was alongside her as she was being prepped to go into the operating room. She was conscious but not totally there because of all the painkillers they'd filled her with. Lying there, her face pale beneath a thin plastic surgical cap, she looked so exhausted and resigned.

As I stood next to the gurney and held her hand, the surgeon, who didn't look a day over twenty-nine, dropped yet another bomb on me. Blanche didn't react because she was in La-La Land, but he said, "Mister Phelan, I'm almost certain she's going to need two surgeries."

"Oh no! What are you talking about? You can't be serious. She's going to have to go through this twice? Why?"

The curly-haired doctor with studious brown eyes and the build of a marathoner said, "From what I've seen in the X-rays, your wife's ankle is so badly shattered and splintered that I'm probably going to have to install a brace to hold it together for a week. Then, yes, she will have to come back for the reconstructive surgery."

This nightmare was only getting worse. I was almost as tired as Blanche and looked just about as bad.

"Doc, listen to me. This woman is one of the finest human beings alive. I'm not saying this just because she's my wife, but believe me; this is a very special woman lying here. Can't you please *try* to do the reconstruction right now?"

Both his young face and his words told me he was somewhat offended when he said, "Of course, if it is possible I'll do it right now. But she's had a very serious compound break. I'm almost certain that the tissue surrounding the bones will be badly damaged. That's why we have to hold everything together with a brace for awhile . . . so that the surrounding tissue can heal."

Looking up to the white ceiling now, I let out a long weary breath. Then I looked back at him.

"What kind of brace are we talking about here? You're not going to put one of those nasty looking ones with all those nail-like things going into her skin, are you?"

"Yes, there will be pins involved. I'm sorry, but I have to do what's necessary."

"What are the odds you'll have to do that?"

Looking a bit testy again he said, "There's probably only about a five-percent chance I *won't* have to, Mister Phelan. I've done a considerable number of these surgeries, and as I told you last night, this is one of the worst breaks I've ever seen. I'm sorry, but we have to go into surgery now."

He nodded to the two nurses who'd been standing by, and as they prepared to roll Blanche away, I kissed her ever so gently on the lips. Then my voice cracked as I whispered in her ear, "I love you, Blanchie."

"Please," I said looking back at the doctor, "take good care of her."

He assured me he would, and I asked him how long this was going to take.

"If I install the brace, probably an hour or two; if by some chance I *can* reconstruct, it could take up to four hours."

Then as he adjusted his cap he said, "Alright, I've got to be going. You try to take it easy." Patting my arm he added, "I promise . . . as soon as we're done, I'll meet you in the waiting lounge."

151

I waited in the small dim lounge. I'd forgotten my reading glasses, so I perused one magazine after another without them. I probably drank a half-gallon of coffee as well. Except for about twenty minutes when an old man was in the room, I had the place to myself. Time dragged. I got up a few times and took walks outside around the hospital grounds. I don't drink the hard stuff, but had it not been so early, I would have gone somewhere and had a couple of quick ones to settle myself down. Instead I drank all that coffee and became pretty wired. An hour, two, three, and then four finally passed. I thought that must be good news. The doctor just might be putting Blanche's ankle back together. It sure seemed that way. But when three o'clock rolled around, and it had been five full hours, I really started worrying.

What can be taking so damn long? Please God, don't let there be any complications. What if something is going seriously wrong? I don't like the smell of this. I'll freaking kill myself if anything happens to her. I couldn't go on without her. Ohhh . . . please, help me Ernest. If you can hear me, please . . . .

When I was right in the middle of my plea, the door opened. It was the doctor. He told me he'd been amazed at what good shape the tissue surrounding the ankle had been in. He'd completed the job. There would be no need for a second surgery. I don't know how many times I thanked him before I bolted up to Blanche's room to wait for her.

Late the following afternoon, I brought Blanche home with a new walker and a knee-high, inflatable medical boot. With the protective black monstrosity looking like something only a masochistic robot might wear, I knew right off that more adjustments than I'd bargained for would be necessary around our house.

For the next eight weeks, Blanche could not go to work. She only got out of her recliner when she had to. And every time she did, the "clickity-clack, clickity clack" of her four-legged walker was to me a cruel reminder of our worsening situation. Without her working, we were now unable to make even the minimum payments on our burgeoning credit card balance. The excellent rating we'd always managed to maintain took a serious clobbering. And for the first time in our lives we had collection agencies calling us.

I could no longer just run my business. I had to do all the chores at home as well. I knew nothing about cooking and didn't want to learn, but I had no choice. I made breakfast, lunch, and dinner every day. I did the laundry, the cleaning, the dishes and everything else, including helping Blanche in and out of the shower. Around the clock—twenty four/seven—a strangling feeling of impending doom was squeezing away what small semblance of hope we had left. And on top of it all, we hadn't heard a single thing from Amber Rinaldi.

Then one night in late May things got even worse.

It was going on eight o'clock. *Jeopardy* had just ended. Sitting in her recliner with her right ankle full of sheet metal and screws and propping it up with a pillow, Blanche asked me, "Did you get the mail today?"

"No. I didn't," I answered. "I'll get it now."

I didn't get right up. I hesitated a moment and looked at her. She'd put on weight, and that wasn't like her. She'd always taken impeccable care of herself. My wife, the eternal optimist, was now as defeated as I was. A second chin had begun to form beneath her first one. It wasn't all that noticeable, but it was there. She didn't wear makeup anymore; didn't polish her nails; and the only clothes she would wear were my old, baggy tee shirts. I wasn't sure, but I also thought she was becoming a bit dark under her eyes.

I looked down to the three long vertical scars on her ankle and knew well and good they certainly hadn't done anything for her ego.

"I'll be right back," I said lifting myself from the chair.

As I walked across the lawn in dusk's gentle pink light, I stared at the spot where that small depression had been. The thin sandy outline around the clump of grass I'd dug up and filled was still visible. The spot looked like a scar itself—a wound that had caused so much pain and unhappiness. I sneered at it as I made my way to our curbside mailbox.

When I sat back down inside the house, I handed the four or five letter-sized envelopes to Blanche. "Here! You look at them. I can't take any more bad news."

As she opened each envelope, I stared at the TV but saw nothing.

"Oh hell," she said, "you're not going to like this."

Tired as my feet were, I started untying my sneakers. "Alright, Blanche . . . what is it now?"

"It's from one of the banks we have a credit card with. They're raising our interest rate because we've been late."

"To what? How much are they raising it?"

"From twelve percent to *thirty point five percent.* My God, Jack, what are we going to do?"

I sat there speechless and let it sink in. The hot anger within me was building like a volcano about to blow. I was going to scream, pace around the room, throw my hands up in the air and curse a blue streak. I was going to go into a diatribe about how criminal it was to demand such a usurious interest rate. I was going to go into the evils of the banks that were legally indenturing us.

But I didn't because the phone rang. I shot up out of the chair and stormed across the room to put an end to its grating ring.

"Hello!" I snapped. "Who is it?"

I couldn't believe my ears. It was a sales call. Some guy was trying to sell me an alarm system. I cut him short and asked him his name. He told me it was Raymond, and I said, "Raymond, I'll tell you what. Why don't you give me your home phone number? And I'll call you back when you're trying to eat dinner or relax after a hard day."

I then slammed the phone down and couldn't move. I just stood there by the end table and unlit lamp. Finally, I'd had it. I had reached the very end. There was no fight left in me. I just wanted to die. I felt a huge swell of tears building and dropped my head. My shoulders started bouncing. I was totally broken.

Then the phone rang again.

I thought that if it was that Raymond character again and if he had the audacity to call back, I wouldn't even have tried to give him hell. I'd just hang up the phone. I'd disconnect the jack and go to bed. I only wanted to escape now. I just wanted to go to sleep.

But it wasn't the solicitor. It was Amber Rinaldi. And I couldn't believe the excitement in her voice. After exchanging hellos she said, "Jack, I am so happy to tell you that we've just about sold your book."

I took a deep breath. Tilting my head way back, I fought back the tears the best I could. "Oh my God, Amber, I love you." I said.

Then with the first tear finding its way down my cheek, I turned to Blanche. She was sitting up in her recliner now, on the very edge of the cushion. I asked Amber three quick questions. "Who bought it? Which publisher? Is there an advance of any kind?"

"Well, Jack, like I said, we've *just about* sold it."

For the second time in my life my heart stopped. I couldn't believe my ears. She wasn't going to take this away from me, was she? Like everything else in my life, I thought for sure there was now going to be a snag. But I was wrong.

"I'm saying we've *just about* sold it because it's going up for auction next Friday."

"Auction? What do you mean by auction, Amber?"

"Well, when we submit manuscripts to publishers, we usually don't send just one out at a time. I had so much faith in your book that I sent out six—to the six largest publishers in the industry. Four of those have agreed to participate in an auction next week. And that's not all. This is the best part, Jack. Are you ready for it?"

For the first time in a long, long time, a small smile rose on my face. Still struggling to fight back those tears, I could now feel my lips quivering. Nodding at Blanche, I managed to say, "Sure, Amber. Go ahead. I'm definitely ready for the good part."

"Okay. I hope you're sitting down because the bidding is starting at *five-hundred-thousand dollars*."

I couldn't believe my ears. With my eyes gone buggy and still glued to Blanche's, I slowly said, "Half-a-million-dollars! Amber, come on, please, don't do this to me. Don't tell me this is some kind of joke."

"It isn't a joke, Jack. I would never do that to you or anyone else. But listen closely. I said that the bidding is only *starting* at that number. Mister Sheehan and I believe that *The Real Ernest Hemingway* will bring at least a million-two, maybe as much as a million-and-a- half. Jack, your book is going to be big. And remember, we're only talking about the advance here."

"A million-two at least, and that's only the advance?" I said looking at Blanche's beaming, tearful face. "I don't know how to thank you, Amber. My God, you're the greatest. Don't mind me. I don't know what else to say. I am absolutely dumbstruck."

"Why don't I let you go now? Go share the good news with Mrs. Phelan. Enjoy the rest of the evening. I'll call you Monday and fill you in on all the rest of the details."

When we hung up seconds later, Blanche had already started across the room. Clickity-clack, clickity-clack, she worked her way toward me.

I just stood there staring at her and shaking my head in disbelief. When she reached where I was standing, she took one hand off the walker, put it around the back of my neck and pulled my head forward. Eye to eye now and just inches away, we looked at each other in silence. Then she said in a tone slightly louder than a whisper, "You did it, Jack Phelan. You did it."

For another moment we looked at the indescribable relief in each other's eyes. We savored it. We bathed in it. Our incredible dream had finally come true. Then Blanche's eyes widened like I hadn't seen since the day I asked her to marry me. They brightened so much I could no longer see the hint of dark rings I'd suspected. She screamed, "YOU DID IT, JACKY! DAMNED IT, YOU DID IT!" She then took her other hand off the walker and threw both her arms around me. I supported her with mine, and we kissed long and hard.

I felt like we'd just risen from the darkest trench in the deepest ocean. It felt as if we'd been anchored down there for months and had been fighting to hold our breaths. And now, at the very last possible second, we'd broken from our chains. It were as if side-by-side, hand-in-hand, and with a trail of bubbles flowing from both our mouths, we'd torpedoed to the surface. We were now finally above water, and the air was sweet and delicious.

So elated were we that, after we kissed, we didn't even go back to our comfortable recliners. Right there next to the phone, we lowered ourselves onto the sofa. And except to refresh our celebration drinks, we didn't get up for well over an hour. Facing each other with smiles that wouldn't fade, we sat there and talked.

When I told Blanche we could pay off all the bills and get my missing tooth replaced, she only laughed. Shaking her head she said, "Jack, we can have *anything* we want. Even after the agency gets fifteen percent, we're still going to get *a million dollars.*" Then she slowly repeated, "A-million-dollars, Jack! And that's only the advance! Sure, we'll have to pay some steep taxes, but you know how we are. We don't spend much. We'll have more than enough to move up to New England like we've wanted to for so long. We can get that little log house in Maine we've dreamed about. We'll have property and animals. You can buy yourself a new truck. You can work on another book."

Pausing then, she put her hand on my knee. One more joyous tear formed on her eyelash. It tumbled to her cheek as she said, "My God, Jack, can you imagine? For once in our lives we won't have to worry."

Later on when it came time to go to bed, I went to the kitchen and got two glasses of ice water like I always had. With her cumbersome walker, Blanche made her way down the hallway toward the bathroom. Slow as she was, I went around her on my way to the bedroom.

157

I put one glass of water on her nightstand, went around to the other side of the bed, and put the other on the small empty space in front of my lamp. Then I walked back to the bathroom.

Blanche was spreading toothpaste onto our brushes. As she handed me mine, she said, "Ernest is going to be so proud of you."

"I hope so," I said. "After all, that's why I was allowed to come back . . . to write that book. I can't wait to tell him the good news."

"Who knows? He might already know."

"Maybe, but I'm going to tell him anyway."

I finished brushing before Blanche did and went back into the bedroom. Standing at the foot of the bed and about to pull my tee shirt over my head to get ready to take a shower, I suddenly got a very strange feeling. For some reason my eyes were pulled towards my nightstand. Still holding the bottom of my shirt in both hands and squinting toward the lamp's dim light, I noticed something there that minutes earlier hadn't been. I took one step closer, and I froze in my tracks. At first I was stunned by what was lying in front of my water glass, but then I smiled. It was a pencil. It was small, almost sharpened down to a stub. And it was green.

CPSIA information can be obtained at www.ICGtesting.com
Printed in the USA
LVOW012023240613

340000LV00023B/1327/P